Praise for *Virtuosity*

"An intoxicating blend of passion, vulnerability, and the desire to have it all, no matter the cost. A mesmerizing read."

—Lauren Myracle, bestselling author of *Shine* and *ttyl*

"Passionate and true, *Virtuosity* sings from first page to last."

—Sarah Ockler, author of *Bittersweet*
and *Twenty Boy Summer*

"Beautiful writing, a swoon-worthy romance, and tension that will keep you turning the pages. *Virtuosity* is pitch-perfect."

—Lauren Barnholdt, author of
The Thing About the Truth and *Two-Way Street*

★ "Martinez brings this overwrought world to tense, quivering life and guides readers through it confidently. A brilliant debut."

—*Kirkus Reviews*, starred review

"Riveting. . . . A beautifully written story."

—*SLJ*

Also by Jessica Martinez

The Space Between Us

Virtuosity

jessica martinez

Simon Pulse

New York London Toronto Sydney New Delhi

SIMON PULSE

An imprint of Simon & Schuster Children's Publishing Division
1230 Avenue of the Americas, New York, NY 10020
First Simon Pulse paperback edition September 2012
Copyright © 2011 by Jessica Martinez
All rights reserved, including the right of reproduction
in whole or in part in any form.
SIMON PULSE and colophon are registered trademarks
of Simon & Schuster, Inc.
Also available in a Simon Pulse hardcover edition.
For information about special discounts for bulk purchases,
please contact Simon & Schuster Special Sales at 1-866-506-1949
or business@simonandschuster.com.
The Simon & Schuster Speakers Bureau can bring authors
to your live event. For more information or to book an event contact
the Simon & Schuster Speakers Bureau at 1-866-248-3049
or visit our website at www.simonspeakers.com.
Designed by Mike Rosamilia
The text of this book was set in Janson Text LT.
Manufactured in the United States of America
2 4 6 8 10 9 7 5 3 1
The Library of Congress has cataloged the hardcover edition as follows:
Martinez, Jessica.
Virtuosity / Jessica Martinez. — 1st Simon Pulse hardcover ed.
p. cm.
Summary: Just before the most important violin competition of
her career, seventeen-year-old prodigy Carmen faces critical decisions
about her anti-anxiety drug addiction, her controlling mother,
and a potential romance with her most talented rival.
ISBN 978-1-4424-2052-6 (hc)
[1. Violin—Fiction. 2. Musicians—Fiction. 3. Mothers and
daughters—Fiction. 4. Competition (Psychology)—Fiction.
5. Conduct of life—Fiction. 6. Drug abuse—Fiction. 7. Chicago (Ill.)—Fiction.]
I. Title.
PZ7.M36715Vir 2011
[Fic]—dc22
2010042513
ISBN 978-1-4424-2053-3 (pbk)
ISBN 978-1-4424-2054-0 (eBook)

For my parents,
Gary and Wendie Low,
who taught me
to love music and books.

The balcony felt cold under my cheek. Ten floors below me the traffic of Lake Shore Drive purred, but it seemed miles away. Everything before me was perfectly still: a black starless sky over Lake Michigan, my bare arm jutting out between metal bars, and the burnt-orange scroll of my violin rising out of my clenched fist.

It would be as easy as opening my hand. I could just uncurl my fingers one by one, and when the last one relaxed, the violin would slice the night sky like a blade, plummeting to the ground below. Then it would be over.

I exhaled and felt my body flatten against the concrete. Diana would be furious about the gown. Her personal dressmaker had twisted and tucked and pleated the filmy chiffon until it looked like a waterfall, flowing cascades in three shades of blue. Now it was bunched beneath me, probably soaking up dirt, grease, cigarette ash, and whatever else hotel balconies collected.

I shivered. The wind swirled around me, picking up my hair and whipping it against my cheek and bare back. The hair clips and bobby pins were long gone— they'd been the first things I'd removed after stepping inside the hotel room. Then I'd slipped off my heels, peeled off my stockings, and pulled out my earrings. But nothing helped. I couldn't slough off the shame that clung to my skin.

So I took my violin onto the balcony.

I still felt the jaws of this nightmare locked around me, the tension twisting in my chest, my head, my calves, my fingers.

1.2 million.

That was how much the violin was worth. But the figure was hard to understand. Hard to *feel*. I let the violin sway, just a little, and closed my eyes. *Murder*. The word came to my mind and I dismissed it. That was ridiculous. The violin wasn't a baby or an animal. It wasn't living.

But that would be easier to believe if I hadn't felt it breathe and sing.

I opened my eyes. My knuckles, bony and white, were shaking. The pills were wearing off. The music was over. I opened my hand.

Chapter 1

Carmen, stop staring. You can't force him to appear with your eyes," Heidi said.

She was right. But I couldn't risk missing him either. The backstage door of the Chicago Symphony Center was frozen shut, and it had been for at least a half hour. He had to be coming out soon.

"Trade you," she said.

I took a quick glance at my dessert, a miniature chocolate cake with a molten center oozing out and a dollop of whipped cream on top. Then I looked at Heidi's, a lemon drop cupcake nestled in an unnaturally yellow cloud of spun sugar. Both were missing one bite.

"What's wrong with yours?" I asked, eyes back on the target.

"Nothing. It's just too tart for me. Look at it, though. Isn't it pretty?" She poked it with her fork.

"Um . . ." I didn't really care. Where was he?

She smiled, sensing victory, and tucked her silky blond hair behind her ears. "I'm just in the mood for something richer." She glanced at my plate again. "And you love lemon, right?"

"I guess." I pushed my plate toward her. I didn't *hate* lemon.

"You're the best," she said, her fork already sinking into my cake.

"I know."

I took a bite of her dessert. The lemon curd *was* tart, especially after that bite of chocolate cake, but the frosting was painfully sweet. Elegant and trendy, like everything else on Rhapsody's menu, but not something I actually wanted to eat.

I took one more bite, then slid the cupcake out of my way and propped my chin on my hands. I had selected the patio's corner table specifically for its view of the backstage entrance to Symphony Center. We were close enough to see the paint peeling off the door, but sufficiently hidden by Rhapsody's hovering gold umbrellas and the fat green leaves sprouting from planters. Perfect for hiding.

"Remind me what I'm looking for again." Heidi licked a chocolate smudge from her thumb.

"Blond hair, violin case."

"Right. Now remind me why you're stalking this mysterious albino violinist."

"He's not an albino and I'm not stalking. Stalking implies some kind of romantic interest."

"Sheesh. Lighten up," she teased. "A little crush doesn't have to be such a big deal."

I wanted to ignore her, but she was just too far off. "Again, Jeremy King is not a crush. I've never even met him. He's the competition."

"But here's the part I don't get: Why do you need to see him? You're a violinist. It's not like you're going to arm wrestle him. What is a visual going to tell you?"

"Nothing. I'm just curious." I pulled my hair up and tried to smooth the mass of unruly curls into a ponytail. "Everybody is talking about this guy."

"Everybody?"

I didn't have to look at her to know she was smirking. My everybody was not her everybody. Occasionally I forgot that the rest of the world didn't exist exclusively in the realm of classical music.

"I think this competition is finally getting to you," she said. "It's so bizarre to see you worried. You never worry."

"I'm not worried," I said. "I just want to see him. And

I've been preparing for the Guarneri Competition for four years now. There would be something wrong with me if I wasn't getting a little freaked out."

Heidi's eyes widened. "Are you going to make a Jeremy King voodoo doll? Is that why we're here?" Then before I could glare at her, she gave me her signature sweet smile.

Heidi's cuteness was her greatest weapon. She used it to win people over, and then, knowing she was too adorable to hate, said and did whatever she felt like. I loved her like a sister, but she drove me nuts. And I had to wonder, if I had baby blue eyes and butter-yellow hair (yes, Heidi was essentially Barbie minus the sexy pout), would I get the same free pass? It'd be nice to be brutally honest, even act like a brat occasionally. But my dark, curly hair and brown eyes just didn't cast the same spell. The slightly oversize nose probably didn't help either.

"No voodoo dolls," I said, "but just think how much more interesting this is than physics or French, which is what we're supposed to be doing right now."

"Agreed."

"Although, I guess that's what my mom is paying you for."

She sat up straight and looked around the patio, as if Diana might actually be lurking behind an umbrella.

"Looking for someone?"

Heidi shrugged. "Nope. Just a reflex."

"We'll do physics and French tomorrow. I'm almost finished anyway."

Heidi couldn't argue with that. They were my last two high school courses. I'd left physics to the end because I hated it, but my test scores were good. Not that it mattered. And French had been an afterthought. It wasn't a GED requirement, but during my European tour last spring I'd fallen in love with the sound of the language, the way the words rolled around and tumbled out.

"You're right," Heidi said. "Spying on lover-boy is more fun anyway."

"I hate you."

"No, you don't." She smiled and ate the last bite of my cake. "I've got an interview, by the way."

"For what?" I asked, without breaking my stare on the door.

"A real job. No offense."

"None taken." I paused. "That's great," I added, trying to sound sincere.

Heidi getting a real job was the inevitable. She had been tutoring me for six years, but now I was almost done, going to Juilliard in the fall. Of course she was interviewing. But for what? She had a degree in art history and *I* was her work experience.

"What kind of job?" I asked.

She shrugged. "Human Resources at OfficeMax."

I nodded.

She nodded.

Neither of us had to say it, but we both were thinking it: She should have gone to dental school.

The server came with a new soda for Heidi and refilled my water.

"Anything else I can get you?" she asked.

Heidi shook her head no, and the server left. My eyes never left the backstage door. It didn't budge.

"So how do you know he has blond hair if you've never seen him before?" Heidi asked.

"His picture," I said. "It's next to his bio in the Carnegie Hall program." I pulled the booklet from the crocheted bag on my lap. The hemp purse was a souvenir I'd bought from Camden Market in London on the last day of my British Isles tour. It was stuffed with CDs—an array of the Bach Violin Sonatas and Partitas recordings. Yuri had sent me home with them after my lesson to listen and dissect.

I handed Heidi the Carnegie Hall program, which flipped open to the exact page. "Diana brought it back from New York."

"She heard him play?"

"No. The program is from a year ago. She just picked it up for me."

"And did she bring it home from New York with the spine split open to this page, or did you do that?"

I ignored the bait. She was either suggesting that Diana was a pressuring stage mom or that I was obsessed with Jeremy King. Neither was entirely true.

Or false.

Heidi examined the picture. "Cute kid. Dimples, curls, he's like a male Shirley Temple. How old?"

"Seventeen."

"No way."

I shrugged. "That's what his bio says."

"More like twelve."

I checked my watch. 1:37. "His rehearsal should have ended at one fifteen. Maybe we missed him."

"How do you know when he rehearses?"

"I saw the CSO rehearsal schedule last week. I had yesterday's noon slot, he was supposed to have today's."

But the door still hadn't opened. At least not since we'd sat down thirty minutes ago, which meant Jeremy had to be still inside.

Heidi picked up the program again and brought the photo closer to her face. "He can't be your age."

I shrugged and looked back at the door. Maybe it was locked, I reasoned. Maybe he'd gone around to one of the front exits, but that was tricky from the backstage dressing rooms if you weren't familiar with the hallways and side entrances and tunnels. No, it would be this door.

Suddenly, the door swung open. I inhaled sharply

before I realized it wasn't him. It was a tall, lanky guy wearing jeans, a T-shirt, a baseball cap. A stage hand, maybe. But there, slung over his shoulder, was a violin case. I squinted into the glare. Why hadn't I brought sunglasses? Blond hair curled up around the back edge of his hat, and under the shadow the bill cast over his face, I could see the dimples that creased his cheeks.

Jeremy King.

My stomach fell. That could *not* be Jeremy King. That was *not* the boy in the photo or the picture I'd seen online. Unless those pictures were old.

Really, really old.

I forced myself to take a slow breath. If that was Jeremy King, he wasn't a child prodigy. At least not anymore.

The guy in the cap—a Yankees cap, I could see now—glanced right and left, trying to orient himself. Then, without warning, he turned and stepped in the least likely direction. Toward me. I had been counting on him cutting through the parking lot and across Wabash for the El station. Instead, he walked along the side of the building over the crumbling parking blocks, toward Rhapsody. He was whistling, and the fingers of his right hand trailed along the red brick as he walked. Long, slow strides propelled him closer and closer to me. I sat frozen, hypnotized by his fluid movement.

I should have looked away. If I'd been thinking, I

would have pretended to drop something or I could have at least rooted around in my purse with my head down. But of course I wasn't thinking.

And then he looked right at me. His eyes locked into mine like two magnets. His face held the blank expression people give strangers in elevators or on sidewalks.

I still could have looked away, while his face was still empty, in that moment before it happened. But I was too stunned. *This* was Jeremy King.

That's when his face changed. His eyes narrowed and his mouth formed a smug grin.

Before I could think, my head jerked down and my hand shot up to cover my face.

"What are you doing?" Heidi hissed.

I'd forgotten she was even there. "Nothing. I don't know." What *was* I doing? "I don't want him to see me."

"Too late, genius," she said.

"Is he still looking at me?"

"Yes. And just because you can't see him doesn't mean he can't see you. Move your hand."

"But he'll know I'm spying on him."

"Trust me, he already knows."

She reached over, took my wrist, and pushed my hand into my lap. I forced my eyes up.

He was still staring at me, not more than ten feet away now, but the grin had become a full-blown sneer. And just when he was close enough that I could have reached out and grabbed his arm, he lifted his hand and saluted me.

I did nothing.

He walked by and was gone.

Heidi and I sat in silence. My stomach churned and I wondered whether those few bites of bitter lemon drop cupcake would come up. Why hadn't I taken my medication? I should have known I would need it.

Heidi spoke first. "Wow."

I heard myself groan.

"That was bad," she added.

"How did that happen? How did he see me? How did he recognize me?"

Heidi shook her head. "Really, Carmen? I mean, it was bad luck that he happened to walk this way, but not that surprising that he recognized you."

"But he's never met me before!"

"Maybe not officially."

"No, not at all," I insisted.

"I could walk into any music store in the country, probably the world, and find a stack of CDs with your face on the cover. Do I need to remind you that you won a Grammy last year? Of course he knows what you look like."

I could barely hear her. My heart was still thundering in my ears.

"Think about it," she continued. "You're scared of him. He's probably scared of you."

I put my cheek on the tabletop and closed my eyes. I needed an Inderal. Why hadn't I brought the pills in my purse? "I'm not scared."

Across the street the El thundered by, making the table buzz beneath my cheek. Even with my eyes closed I could feel Heidi's stare, sense her harshness melting into concern.

"It's just a competition, Carmen," she said softly.

But it wasn't just a competition. Heidi couldn't grasp that and I didn't expect her to. I didn't expect anybody to understand. I wasn't just scared of Jeremy King. I thought about him constantly, googled his name and read his reviews, listened to his CDs, and studied that stupid out-dated photo from the Carnegie Hall program. If I wasn't practicing or thinking about music, I was thinking about Jeremy King. I was obsessed, and I had every reason to be.

Jeremy King could ruin my life.

Chapter 2

I was named after a fiery Spanish gypsy. The real Carmen, if opera characters qualify as real, got into knife fights and seduced matadors and inspired jealous rages. The real Carmen would *not* have tried to hide behind a plant and then, even worse, her hand, when confronted by her nemesis.

I tried not to think about that, or him, that evening as I sat on the front porch swing with my mother, playing the aria game. The rules were simple—she hummed any aria, I had to name the opera it came from—but winning was impossible, since she knew every opera ever written from beginning to end, and, well, I didn't.

"*Don Giovanni?*" I guessed, trying hard to ignore the shame, the sourness that had been curdling in my gut since Jeremy had smiled at me.

"Right composer, wrong opera," she said, and went back to humming. Diana's voice was both shiny and jagged, like crumpled tinfoil. It was the voice of a soprano with scars.

"Just tell me. All of Mozart's operas sound the same."

"I can't believe you said that," she said with mock dismay. She knew they did. She started humming again.

"No really, just tell me," I repeated impatiently. Apparently humiliation made me grumpy.

She narrowed her eyes and her crow's-feet appeared, flaws in an otherwise flawless face. "*Le Nozze di Figaro*," she said. "You look stressed. Here, put your head on my lap and let me play with your hair."

I obeyed, and she started humming something new.

"*Madama Butterfly*," I said. "I really don't feel like playing anymore."

She stopped. We listened to the porch swing creak as she unwound sections of curls with her fingers. Why did I have to be such a brat? She loved this game.

"What's the matter?" she asked after a minute. "Did you and Heidi fight or something?"

"No." I closed my eyes and saw Jeremy's face.

"So it's just the Guarneri then," she said.

I didn't answer. *Just the Guarneri*. The semifinals were in two weeks, and the finals were a couple of days after that. It was the most prestigious competition in classical music, and anything short of first place would be devastating. I was expected to win.

Just the Guarneri.

Diana knew better.

"Let's get you thinking about something else," she said. "Do you want to go to a movie?"

"Not really." I paused, considering her mood. She seemed relaxed, and maybe just eager enough to indulge me. I forged ahead. "Tell me what it was like to sing with the Met."

She sighed, but it sounded more like surrender than frustration. She liked talking about her career. "I've already told you everything, Carmen."

I didn't believe that. Not for a second. "So tell me again."

"Let's see. I'd just moved from Milan to New York, and I didn't know a soul. My English was pretty good, but my accent . . ." She laughed, remembering. "It was so strong I had to repeat everything at least three times. I thought Americans were all hard of hearing."

That part always seemed hard to imagine—my mother the immigrant. Now her accent was light and mostly masked by her gravelly voice. "Go on."

"So. I had been in the States for two months when

I auditioned with the Met and got the position." She paused and took another section of my hair to comb through with her fingers. It felt good. "It was my dream, but my head was spinning so fast it was hard to believe it was real. To go from being a poor student in Milan one day, to lead soprano with the New York Metropolitan Opera Company the next was . . . overwhelming. I'd be lying if I said it didn't go to my head a little. I thought I owned the world." She chuckled. "I *did* own the world."

"What did you sing?" I knew the answer, but did it matter?

"My first season we sang *Aida*, then *La Traviata* and *Tosca*. Second season we sang . . ." She trailed off, waiting for me to fill in.

"*Carmen*."

"Exactly. Then you came along nine months later."

Typically evasive. "Either you left something out or I was the product of immaculate conception."

She sighed dramatically. "You're like a dog with a bone, Carmen. Fine. Jonathon Glenn was in the audience on opening night. His parents had season tickets, box seats if I remember correctly—still do, probably. That's what people in their circle do to show the world how refined they are."

"Or they might just like opera."

"Oh, please. People like the Glenns live for dressing up in sequined gowns and tuxes just so they can see themselves in the society pages. Opera houses are full of them—people who have no idea what opera they are listening to, but who'll drink champagne in the lobby and smile for anyone with a camera."

"All right, tangent explored, go on."

"Where was I?"

"He came to the opening night of *Carmen*."

"Right. And then he came backstage after the performance to meet me. The cast was going out to celebrate, but Jonathon convinced me to go out with him for drinks instead. My friends were annoyed, but I didn't care. He was good-looking and just so . . . I don't know . . . confident. Like he knew I couldn't possibly reject him."

She paused and squinted into the street, or maybe she was squinting back in time. Either way, the crow's-feet reappeared. In the silence I could hear her fighting the familiar battle—trying to decide what to tell and what to keep back. Every time I pushed her to this place she revealed a little more, but I could see in her eyes the weight of things held out of my reach.

"For the next four months we were inseparable. He even came to my rehearsals. At first I was worried that he was going to lose his job because he was with me all the time. Then I discovered you can't get fired from being the only heir to your father's media empire." She took a slow breath through her nose. When she continued it was in a softer voice. "Back then, he was more than his parents, though. He really loved the music, and I thought he really loved me . . ."

"So why four months then?"

The porch swing creaked. She crossed her legs, displacing my head, and I nearly fell off the swing headfirst. That question never made her happy. "We weren't right for each other."

"That's so vague."

"Maybe. But it's the truth."

I sat up and stared at her face. People said we looked alike, but they were wrong. Maybe we had the same almond eyes and curly hair, but she had a delicate nose and fuller lips. She was beautiful.

"It wasn't because of *you*, Carmen. I promise."

"Did he know you were pregnant?"

"It all happened at once. Getting pregnant, breaking up with Jonathon, my diagnosis . . ."

And I'd lost. This was where the story always dead-ended, losing her voice. I knew the pitiful progression: vocal cord polyps led to multiple surgeries, which led to permanent scarring, which led to broken contracts and broken career and broken dreams. Somewhere in there she had a broken heart, too. This was where the fairy tale became a tragedy, and I knew from experience, if I pushed her now she would cry.

"As a musician, you should be able to understand this," she said. "He fell in love with Diana the soprano, but suddenly I wasn't Diana the soprano anymore. I was *just* Diana."

"So he only loved you for your voice?"

"No," she said. "He wasn't a terrible person. He was just young and a bit of a womanizer. Probably still is, but that wasn't the problem. It was me who changed. Imagine if you had to stop playing the violin. You wouldn't be the same person, would you? My life changed overnight, and I was grieving and trying to recover from the botched surgery and then I found out I was pregnant on top of everything. I was a mess."

I'd stopped listening. I was trying to picture myself without violin and saw . . . nothing.

"Let it go, Carmen. I know you're curious about him, but it's a pointless obsession. He will always be too self-absorbed to be any kind of father figure, and you have a dad. You know how much Clark loves you." She paused and continued with the faintest shade of bitterness. "Besides, Jonathon may not be in your life, but his family's money certainly is."

It felt like an insult, even though I knew it wasn't me she wanted to hurl it at. I thought about what the Glenns had done for me and felt vaguely guilty, as if I'd gone begging to them. I hadn't.

At that moment, the SUV drove up. "Ladies," Clark said, climbing the steps with a smile on his face, a briefcase in one hand and flowers in the other.

Diana stood and met him with a kiss, leaving me on the swing.

"Hey, Superman," I said, "how are the tights feeling today?" It was our joke, the one I refused to let die and the one he always had a new response to. As he explained, when your name is Clark and you wear horn-rimmed glasses, you have to develop a healthy database of responses to Superman jabs.

"Itchy. Really itchy."

"Ever think of washing them?"

"Nope. That would be bad luck."

Diana was already holding her flowers and dragging him inside by the arm.

"Come inside with us," Clark said.

"I want to sit out here a while longer. I'll come in when I'm cold."

That wouldn't be long. I could feel the afternoon warmth dissipating in the air around me. The door to the house closed and the sounds outside seemed to grow louder: birds chattering in the newly budding oak trees that lined our street; a bike bell, shrill and sharp; the laughter of two little boys chasing each other down the sidewalk.

Alone, my thoughts became clearer. They always did. For some reason, when Diana was around, my brain was too busy reacting to what she said to function properly, and I ended up pushed into corners and firing at targets for no reason it all.

It didn't make sense, for example, to be bugging Diana with questions about Jonathon right now. With the Guarneri looming, he was the least of my worries. And of course, she was right about not needing him. Clark *was* my dad. I was six when he and Diana had married, which meant there was almost nothing in the pre-Clark memory file.

There was no telling what kind of crazy orbit Diana and I would be spinning into if he hadn't come along. Clark balanced us out. He was *not* a musician, *not* intense, *not* competitive—basically the yin to our yang. Clark cooked gourmet food. And he watched the weird indie films with me and boring dramas with Diana, even though I knew he'd rather be overdosing on one of his dorky sci-fi series.

I barely knew Jonathon Glenn. When I was little, visits had been sporadic and forced. Hardly memorable. I remembered a few lame outings, like an awkward walk in Central Park followed by a visit to some bookstore. Now the visits were pretty much nonexistent. He split his time between London and Beijing, or wherever else work took him, and called on my birthday. Sometimes. I hadn't seen him for four years, and we hadn't talked since the Christmas before last.

I shivered and pulled my sweater around me. I couldn't wait until summer. Just a couple more weeks and it would stay warm into the evening, and the Guarneri would be over. Almost summer. Almost over. I stood up and went inside.

Chapter 3

That night, I lay in bed and tortured myself by replaying every brutal second of the Rhapsody fiasco until my stomach ached. Stupid Heidi, stupid lemon drop cupcake, stupid Jeremy King, stupid me. My room was too hot, my tank top had twisted itself nearly backward, and the comforter scratched my legs every time I moved. Or didn't move. Maybe this was what hell was like, insomnia-fueled misery.

My bedside clock said 2:21 when I finally gave up, untangled myself from my sheets, and sat down at my desk. My computer whirred softly as I brought it to life and checked my inbox. One unread email sat at the top of the list, bolded. The subject line read, *nice to meet you too*. I didn't recognize the sender's address, jk45@yehudimenuhinschool.co.uk, but it had the mixed up look of foreign spam. I needed another hard drive clean-out and lecture from Clark about opening strange email like I needed a kick in the head. I selected it and let the cursor hover over the delete button for just a second. And then another second. Something in my brain turned, like a puzzle piece rotating into place. If I could stretch those letters apart there was something recognizable there. Yehudi Menuhin School. It was the most exclusive violin academy in England, possibly all of Europe. It was Jeremy's school. Crap.

I opened the email.

Carmen,

Normally I would feel a little awkward emailing someone I'd never met and who hadn't actually even given me her email address, but you were the one on a stakeout today, so if one of us should be embarrassed. . . . By the way, the CSO receptionist is more than happy to give out your contact info to anyone claiming to be a fan.

I'm curious—are you hunting down all the semifinalists, or just the ones who've got a shot at winning? Is precompetition stalking an American custom? Should I be doing it myself, or does this email qualify? I've always thought practicing scales and slow passage work was the best way to prepare for competitions, but maybe hiding behind bushes with binoculars would be a better use of my time. How is it working out for you?

Jeremy King

P.S. Good luck

I read the email six times. During the first reading I registered shock and shock alone. Second, humiliation. Third, humiliation. Fourth, humiliation with just a glimmer of anger. Then during the fifth and sixth readings the anger grew into rage, and I knew I was done when I was ready to put my fist through my computer screen.

My hands shook as I hit reply and began writing. I didn't need to think about what to write. Fury, as it turned out, made me extra eloquent, or at least extra prolific.

Jeremy King had clearly not been told what an insignificant piece of crap he was lately—maybe ever—and I was just the girl to do it. It would be doing a disservice to him and certainly to humanity, if I didn't cut him down to size. *He* was the one who needed to feel humiliated. Not me. My fingers could barely keep up with the insults my brain spewed. I wrote words I'd never actually said aloud. The feeling was beautiful.

I was several pages into my diatribe before I stopped to breathe. I'd lost sense of time. Sleepless nights usually inched by, but anger had eaten the last hour. Was it really after three already? I read over what I'd written. I sounded . . . insane. Like a ranting lunatic. I couldn't send this. My index finger found the delete key and I watched the insults disappear one letter at a time.

What was his problem? It wasn't like I had done anything malicious—*he* was the one who'd acted like a jerk with that salute. I'd just been embarrassed, but that was clearly a mistake. Jeremy wasn't a nice guy. He was the kind of guy who saw weakness and then scraped at it, hoping to expose something raw and painful he could spit into. The tears were there, behind my eyes. I could coax them out if I concentrated, but crying always left me feeling weak and I didn't want to feel any weaker.

Weakness. He thought I was weak, because that was how I'd acted today. Maybe not responding at all would be better. An egomaniac like that—he'd probably be more annoyed by silence than anything else.

Unless he saw silence as more weakness.

I laced my fingers behind my head and bounced against the back of the chair. I needed to write something simple, something profound but totally void of emotion.

I started again.

Jeremy,

You are an ass.

Carmen

P.S. Good luck to you too.

Much better. Before I could talk myself out of it, I pressed send, a thrill running up my spine. Had I really just done that? It was so un-Carmen.

I didn't even glance at my bed. It would take a combination of hypnosis and a fistful of sedatives to make my brain submit to sleep right now. Instead, I tiptoed across the hall to my practice studio. Tiptoeing wasn't necessary. From the top of the stairs I could hear Clark snoring—his usual choking, guttural grunt-fest—which meant Diana's earplugs were in place.

My violin case lay waiting on the floor in the center of the room, propped against the maple music stand. With just the moonlight from the window to see by, I crouched, unzipped the cover, and began the ritual preparation: unlatching the Velcro neck strap, attaching the shoulder rest, twisting the screw at the base of the bow to tighten the horsehair.

Just enough light shone in the window for the violin to glow. The amber wood formed graceful arcs and points, its grain darkened by centuries of being touched and played. It was still hard to believe it was mine.

They had bought it for me. The Glenns. This was what my father was good for. Money. For the first twelve years of my life I had been the irritating detail Thomas and Dorothy Glenn hoped would disappear if they just ignored me long enough. I was the unfortunate byproduct of a fling between their playboy son and some opera singer, of all things, a woman just Catholic enough to refuse an abortion, or too much of a gold digger. According to Diana, anyway.

But then I turned sixteen and everything started happening quickly, too quickly for me to dissect and make sense of. I won the Grammy for best classical album and a week later my face appeared on the cover of *Time* magazine with the words "Virtuosity in America" underneath it. Right after the *Time* article, *Vanity Fair* did an interview and photo shoot, and that was when Dorothy Glenn called to congratulate me.

Diana had thrust the phone into my hands and shrugged as if to say *good luck*. I didn't know what to say. I hadn't seen or talked to her since I was five, and the birthday notes— cards featuring mountain landscapes and bouquets of freesia and other stuff little girls don't care about—had stopped at age nine. Was she trying to pretend we were close?

I didn't even recognize her voice. "We are so proud of you," she said.

I didn't say what I was thinking, which was that I wasn't really hers to be proud of.

After a fascinating discussion of the weather, she saved us both from any more pretending and moved on to the reason for her call. "Your grandfather and I have been discussing an investment and I wanted to consult you." The stiffness in her voice had relaxed into something closer to smugness.

"With me? I'm probably the wrong person to ask about investing."

"No, dear. You are definitely the right person." She paused for what sounded like dramatic effect, but it was lost on me. I had no clue where she was going. "We've been thinking about purchasing the Gibson Stradivarius. Have you heard of it? It's coming up for auction at Christie's next month."

A Stradivarius. The Gibson Stradivarius. Yes, I'd heard of it—it was one of the best violins in the world. At auction, the cheapest Strads were going for at least half a million dollars. The Gibson would go for a lot more because of its tone. It was one of the sweetest sounding violins ever crafted. In comparison, the perfectly respectable twelve thousand dollar German instrument I played was a tin box.

"Of course, we want *you* to play it."

The silence that followed was thick with expectations. Dorothy probably expected a gasp, followed by confessions of my undying gratitude. What she got was the sound of the phone hitting the wooden floor and then bouncing down the stairs, followed by me scrambling after it.

"What on earth was that?" she said, once I'd picked the phone up again.

"Sorry," I said, struggling to catch my breath. "I dropped the phone."

"Well, let's hope you keep a tighter grip on the new violin."

After we hung up I screamed. I was laughing, and then crying, and then jumping on the couch in Diana's office and laughing and crying at the same time. "She called it an investment," I said after I'd calmed down enough to talk, "like she was talking about buying property on Martha's Vineyard or shares in Microsoft or something. I wanted to yell, '*Do you even have any idea what you're buying?*'"

"Carmen, *you* don't have any idea what they're buying."

"What are you talking about? Didn't you hear me? They're buying the Gibson Strad!"

"Wrong." She pushed her chair away from her desk, took off her glasses, and chucked them onto the pile of receipts in front of her. "They're buying you."

The first time I played it, I knew. It had always been a part of me. I hadn't realized I was incomplete, but the experience was one of coming home. Or of being whole. My body welcomed its weight and the way it nestled perfectly under my jaw; my ear recognized its voice as *my* voice. It always had been.

That had been a year ago, but holding it up under the moonlight, I still couldn't believe the violin was mine to play. The Glenns ended up paying $1.2 million for it. Or as Diana said, $1.2 million for *me*. But as much as she disliked the situation, she didn't suggest I refuse it either. That was never even a possibility. That would be insane.

I couldn't hate the Glenns the way Diana did. Not anymore, but not just because of the Strad. It was embarrassing, but even though I hadn't been worth acknowledging before I was famous, even though I knew their respect and their gift were more about their status than about me, a small part of me was happy. It wasn't complicated. I wanted them to like me.

But I couldn't tell Diana that. In her world, talent was the only currency, and that made the Glenns worthless: They didn't have it themselves, they hadn't recognized it in her, and they had to have the entire world point it out in me before they even acknowledged me as their granddaughter.

I put the violin under my chin.

Being a violinist had been simpler then. More about music, less about stress. I wanted to play something to take me back. Not the Tchaikovsky Violin Concerto or anything else that had been infected with Guarneri anxiety. Just something beautiful.

My eyes fell on the tiny American flag pin on the case strap, a gift from Clark before my first European tour. I brought violin to shoulder, bow to string, and the opening notes of *Amazing Grace* filled the room. I didn't even have to try. The pressure melted away under the warmth of the melody, and the music spoke. *Forget Jeremy King, forget the competition, forget everyone's expectations.* And by the end of the verse, I almost had.

I put the violin back in its case and tiptoed back across the hall. My bed was suddenly softer, the covers enveloping instead of strangling. Sleep seemed almost attainable.

I was almost there when Diana's ringtone sounded. Just once.

The numbers on the digital face of my bedside clock glowed 3:49. Who would be calling in the middle of the night? I was out of bed and twisting my doorknob as quietly as I could before I thought through the possibilities.

The *pat-pat* of Diana's bare feet on the hardwood floor traveled down the hall and stopped right below me. I fell into a crouch instinctively, just in case she glanced up. She didn't. She turned to face the wall and sat on the bottom step.

"Why are you calling?" Her voice was somewhere between hiss and whisper. "I *told* you not to."

Silence.

The anger was gone when she whispered again. "It's worse. At least according to Yuri . . ."

I leaned forward, but there was nothing to hear. Seconds felt like minutes.

"You're right. It's time . . . I agree. . . . No, *you* work out the details. Isn't wiring money what you do?"

The sharp taste of blood filled my mouth and I realized I'd been biting my lip.

"Let me know when it's taken care of," she said.

She snapped the phone shut, but she didn't stand. She just sat, her shoulders rising and falling gently in the dark.

My calves burned from crouching. They'd give out

soon. I wanted to stand, but if she turned and saw me now, she'd know I'd heard the whole thing. And clearly, she didn't want to be heard.

My mind pulled at the loose threads of her conversation, but everything was too short, too slick to grip. Why did she need money? According to my violin instructor, Yuri—what had she said was according to Yuri? Who was she talking to?

My legs were on fire. I closed my eyes and concentrated on not falling.

Finally, she stood. Her usually perfect posture had wilted into something less than elegant. She looked limp as she walked out of my view, back to Clark's snoring.

I stood and clutched the door frame as a wave of light-headedness washed over me. My brain ached. Something was very wrong. I closed my eyes and tried to hear *Amazing Grace*, but the melody was gone.

Chapter 4

I woke up the next morning with an overwhelming urge to pray. I wasn't particularly religious, unless going to mass on Christmas and Easter and when Nonna visited from Milan counted. In fact, I wasn't even sure if I believed in God. But I didn't specifically *not* believe in God, so erring on the side of caution seemed smart.

Certain dire situations had a way of bringing out the Catholic girl hiding several layers down, and the Guarneri was the definition of dire. The problem was, I couldn't ask for exactly what I wanted. If there *was* a God, I highly doubted he gave the less-than-devout exactly what they wanted. It seemed more respectful, more realistic, to skip the praying to win and just pray to injure myself. *Please God, break my arm. A nice, clean fracture that would require a few months in a shoulder-to-wrist cast to heal completely. Amen.*

I said the Lord's Prayer, or what I could remember of it, and crossed myself, just to make the request more official. Would God punish me for not remembering what I'd only sort of been taught when I was just a little girl by an Italian grandmother who could barely speak English? Maybe. I didn't know.

I did know the Guarneri Competition was something only God, if He existed, could spare me from. Four years ago I'd sat in the audience for the final gala concert, know-ing I was peering into my future. Diana had sweet-talked an old symphony friend into two eighth-row seats, too close for good acoustics but perfect for the view. The violinists' faces shone with sweat under the stage lights. Sometimes, for concentration, they closed their eyes, but when they were open they held all the intensity of the music. Every emotion—elation, anger, grief, love—was magnified under those lights. I should have been watching their technique, but I couldn't stop looking at their faces.

Three finalists performed their concertos with the Chicago Symphony Orchestra, then the judges deliber-ated while the audience waited. And waited. For forty-five minutes Diana circulated and chitchatted with people in the industry, while I mangled my program with sweaty hands and tried to smile at everyone who told me I looked exactly like my mother for the millionth time. How could people socialize right now? Weren't they nervous?

When the results were finally announced I cried. I couldn't help it. Luckily, the applause was noisy and I caught the sob in my throat before it escaped. It wasn't because I was happy for the winner, or sad for the other two competitors who were standing on the stage with plastic smiles over broken faces.

I'd cried because I knew it had to be me next time.

But back then, I was nobody. A thirteen-year-old wonderkid, but those are a dime a dozen. Every city in the world has a best young violinist, and every five years or so they have to get a new one. Musical prodigies almost always settle into lives as musically stifled professionals. Symphonies are full of them.

The Guarneri grand prize is one of the best in classical music: fifty thousand dollars, the four-year loan of the 1742 Guarneri del Gesu violin, and performance opportunities with symphonies all over the world. Most violinists would kill for the Guarneri violin and the cash, but it was the performing opportunities that meant the most to me.

Yuri was right. He always was, despite the thick Ukrainian accent and unnatural syntax. "*This* is one," he had said as I was packing up my violin at the end of my last lesson. "Win Guarneri and you are legend. Lose, and who are you?"

Another time he had told me that people thought Paganini, the nineteenth-century Italian violinist, was possessed by the Devil. "Too good," he said. "People say he is not just man. He has devil." Here he stopped and pointed an arthritic finger at me. "Pray to God for devil like that. And you should know, Paganini played a Guarneri violin."

Yuri could pray for devils. I'd pray for deliverance. *Please God, a nice clean ulna fracture, please. Thy will be done, kingdom come, I think. Amen. And Hail Mary.*

I sat up and looked out my window, only to receive a sharp slap from reality, Chicago-style: an April snowstorm. I stood, walked over to the window, and pulled the curtain aside. Flurries floated by the windowpane, settling on a carpet of snow already muddied by boots and tires. That meant I'd be trekking through the slush to Yuri's apartment for my lesson. It was a four-minute walk to the El station, followed by an eight-minute train ride, and another two minutes on foot—long enough for my feet to get good and wet. I laced up a pair of boots, pulled on a jacket, and slung my violin case onto my back. So much for spring.

Before I left the room, I checked my email. Nothing from Jeremy. Good. He must have agreed with my assessment of him.

According to my clock, I had forty-five minutes until my lesson. I opened the wooden pillbox on my bedside table and took out two tiny orange pills. One at a time, I washed them down with water, and then as an after-thought, I took one more. Better safe than sorry.

It was supposed to take a little while for the Inderal to kick in, but I could feel the difference right away. My palms dried. My breathing slowed. Then that jittery buzz at the base of my skull melted away, and the nausea pressing on my stomach lifted so gradually I couldn't pinpoint the exact moment it vanished, only that it was gone. I loved that part. And once the nervousness had completely disappeared and the flatness descended, it seemed like the whole world took on a matte finish. No gloss to slip on.

Inderal was only supposed to be for performances, but today's lesson was important. I had no problem justifying a couple of pills before the most crucial lesson of the year.

Our house was a textbook row house, tall and skinny and attached to neighbors on both sides. To get to the street, I had to go from my room on the third floor, down a flight of stairs, past the kitchen and the master bedroom, then down another flight of stairs, and past the living room and Diana's office.

Clark's voice met me before I was halfway down the

first flight of stairs. "Fried egg?" he asked. I walked into the kitchen to find him standing at the stove with his back to me, tending an egg with his spatula.

I took a poppy seed bagel from the bread box. "No time."

He shook his head and gently folded the egg over onto itself. "Protein, Carmen. Protein. Those carbs are going to give out halfway through your lesson."

"That's where the Red Bull comes in," I said, taking a can from the fridge door.

"That can't possibly sit well this early in the morning."

I shrugged.

"Are you still planning on going for a run with me tonight?" he asked.

"If you can make it okay with the powers that be. I'm rehearsing with the CSO tomorrow for Saturday night's concert."

"I'll talk to her," he said.

Clark was the only person in my universe who didn't know I was violin girl. To him, it was just another piece of information about me, like my favorite TV show, or my hair color. He was an accountant. He could leave work at work.

I was halfway out of the kitchen when I noticed the basket, wrapped in a flourish of cellophane and curled ribbon. "Where'd this come from?" I asked.

"Sony Classical. It's for you. Follow-up from your mom's meeting with them yesterday, I'm assuming."

I pulled open the packaging and rifled through the bags of specialty foods: white chocolate-dipped apricots, wasabi almonds, Scottish shortbread, mocha truffles. I decided on the apricots and waved them at Clark.

"I'm out."

He waved the spatula in the air. "Give Yuri a big, fat hug and tell him it's from me."

I laughed. Yuri had been my teacher for thirteen years. We'd never hugged. To my knowledge, Yuri had never hugged anyone.

Chapter 5

The train jounced and swayed as the familiar city shapes sped by. I made this trip twice a week, and knew the exact order and location of every building, sign, and fire hydrant along the route. I closed my eyes, enjoying the feel of the train swinging back and forth on the elevated track. It was soothing, but a little sinister too, like a giant snake rolling from side to side.

I was on my way to get yelled at. It wasn't a good feeling, but it wasn't full-blown dread either. I got chewed out too often to actually be scared. Not that it happened at *every* lesson, but with two weeks until the competition, it was pretty much a given. How well I played wouldn't even factor in.

Two weeks.

The train jerked left, and the girl across from me giggled. She and her boyfriend were not making out, but wanting to. They wore private school uniforms: plaid skirt and knee socks for her, dress pants and plaid tie for him, matching blazers with a coat of arms crest for both, though hers was slung over her backpack on the ground in front of her. She was practically sitting on his lap, and he was playing with her earring, a dangly silver thing with loops and beads, while she drew circles on his knee with her finger.

I examined the puddles of melted snow on the toes of my boots so I wouldn't have to watch. Not that they would have noticed. They were my age, but somehow . . . not. School. It had to be school that made them so different. Or not going to school that made me so different. Not that I was a weirdo or anything.

I gave them one last glance. It wasn't just school. My life bore no resemblance to theirs. They weren't worried about anything bigger than algebra tests. I lifted my toes and the puddles spilled off my shoes onto the rubber mats.

The packet. It called. I unzipped the music flap on my case, and fished around for it. Held together by a single staple, the pages were starting to come loose and the corners curled. I'd read it at least twenty times. The papers' edges were starting to split. I flipped to the list of semifinalists and read through the names again.

The twenty names could be categorized a million different ways. Thirteen men and seven women. Nine Americans, six Europeans, four Asians, and a lone Australian. Five teenagers and fifteen twenty-somethings. Eighteen hopefuls, two real contenders.

I turned to the schedule. Each of us had been randomly plugged into a time slot over the two days of semifinals. I had Tuesday two-thirty. Jeremy had Wednesday five o'clock.

When the packet first arrived and I told Yuri about my early slot, he had shrugged and muttered something angry in Ukrainian. And then, in English, "Tuesday sucks."

Typical pep talk.

Yuri Petrov was many things—genius, tyrant, mentor, reality TV addict—but he was not a cheerleader.

Physically, Yuri resembled a troll. Wiry gray hair sprouted from everywhere except the top of his mole-covered head, bruise-colored bags hung below his eyes, and he had a pronounced hunchback. Actually, pronounced was an understatement. His back rose higher than his head, making him look like a human question mark.

When I was fourteen he made me drive him across the city in search of his favorite pipe tobacco (Smoker

Friendly Vanilla Cavendish instead of "the crap brand sold at corner store"). He didn't care that I didn't have a license. He didn't care that I didn't know how to drive, either. I gave in when he threatened to get behind the wheel. He'd just had double cataract surgery.

And then there was the time last year when he'd made me drink vodka until I was drunk, just so I could really understand Shostakovich, and all Russian composers for that matter, as well as the importance of saving celebratory drinking until after performances. I vaguely remembered him saying, "Friends don't let friends drink and get onstage." Then I watched *Dancing with the Stars* sideways, my head on his couch. He drove me home that night and handed me over to Diana with a shrug for an explanation. Diana didn't bat an eye. With talent came eccentricity and she made allowances for it. She'd put me to bed, placed a glass of water and a bottle of aspirin on my nightstand, and told Clark I had the stomach flu.

The train lurched and slowed. The couple across from me stood, and I noticed the rings on the girl's hand as she gripped the pole in front of me. She had two, plus a thumb ring. They looked cool: silver with funky oversize gemstones in different colors. I didn't wear rings—taking them all off and putting them all back on again several times a day to practice seemed like too much hassle—but if I did, I'd get ones like that.

The doors opened and she let herself be steered off the train by her boyfriend, his hands on either side of her waist. There was something about her strut. She looked so sure of herself, even being guided through the crowd by her hip bones.

Yuri's was the next stop. I took a deep breath. Mental preparation was everything.

Yuri could be terrifying, but only if I let him, and I didn't do that anymore. I used to cry when he yelled. Shock, shame, anger—I cried from a combination of all three before I realized that crying just made it worse. I was too young to know better then.

The memory of being so easily hurt was humiliating. Being little and fragile and unable to keep the tears from spilling over my cheeks and dripping onto the wood, having to stop and wipe them up with my sleeve, wipe my runny nose too, and then put my violin back up and keep on playing. . . .

Now, it was all a matter of control. I could tune out the insults, the way the fleshy pockets under his eyes turned purplish-red, how his gnarled hands clenched and shook. All that was unimportant. But what he was actually saying about the music—*that* was golden. He always knew exactly what needed to be done.

The train squealed as it slowed. I leaned into it, and the competition schedule slid off my lap and onto the wet floor. A dark water spot bloomed over it and the names bled and blurred. Jeremy's. Even mine.

Yuri's apartment was the last door on the left at the end of a faded green hallway. The parade of food smells from the elevator to his door took me from China to India to Mexico, with steadily growing Ukrainian undertones. Garlic and cabbage trumped the most pungent odors any other cuisine could offer. For Yuri, it was a source of national pride.

I stopped in front of his door and kicked it twice.

Once, years ago, he had pulled the door open and caught me with my knuckles poised, ready to knock. "Never!" he had cried, and grabbed my fist with a purple-veined hand. "You are violinist! Use feet!" and he had demonstrated by kicking the already open door and putting a nickel-size hole in the wall behind it.

The muffled sounds of TV continued. He had to have heard me. I waited a moment and then kicked again. Nothing. Was that a woman crying? What was he watching? Finally, the noise stopped, and the "swish-swish" of his slippers approached from the other side, followed by the clicking of the lock.

The door swung open and he called, "Lock it," over his shoulder, already shuffling back to his recliner and a half-eaten plate of cheese pierogies.

"Rose ceremony," Yuri said, already back in the

recliner, but leaning forward and staring intently at the screen, where a man in a tuxedo was frozen midblink. He unpaused the DVR. The camera cut to a blonde with rubbery looking breasts and mascara dripping down her face. Yuri didn't comment, but nodded his head, as if to confirm that justice was being served.

I crossed the length of the apartment, past the La-Z-Boy and greasy kitchenette and dirty dishes, to the closed door of his music studio. That door separated worlds. Behind it, the air was always cooler. Dinginess surrendered to old-world elegance, clutter to simplicity. I closed the door behind me and looked around. Everything was in its place. The ebony music stand held the center of the room, its ornate back crisscrossed with stretching arms that looked like branches. Floor-to-ceiling bookshelves of dark wood lined all four walls, packed with thousands of scores, millions of notes. Once when I was younger, inspired by a couple of multiplication problems Heidi had thrown at me, I had tried to calculate just how many notes filled the shelves. I started with the average number of notes per line, then line per page, the page per shelf, which is where things got too confusing. And then I started to wonder how many notes had been played in here, or even just how many *I* had played in here. Impossible.

I took out my violin, tuned, played a few scales in case he was listening, and then played the opening of the

Devil's Trill Sonata by Tartini, my back to the closed door. It was the first piece of my semifinal program, the first thing the judges would hear me play. It sounded solid and crisp, each note biting the string just enough at its beginning, then becoming brilliant and sunny with the right speed and width of vibrato. The details were crucial, but they could strangle the music too.

"No Tartini today."

I jumped, nearly dropping my bow.

He shuffled around me and groaned as he lowered himself into the velvet armchair. His arthritic fingers picked an amber pipe by the stem from the rack on his desk. He rubbed the glossy bowl of the pipe in his left palm. "Why so jumpy? Are you stealing things again?" He opened the ornate box beside his pipe rack and rummaged around for his tobacco cube.

Once when I was thirteen he'd caught me trying to borrow his cake of rosin. I'd left mine at home and didn't have enough on my bow. Four years later, I was still not to be trusted.

"Not jumpy. Just focused."

He cleared his throat, unsatisfied, and began to work the tobacco into the pipe with his gnarled thumb. "No Tartini today," he repeated. "Waste of time. You will make the finals. Tartini and Mozart are both good enough. It will all come down to finals."

Jeremy's face appeared again, the sneer, the arrogant stride.

Yuri lit the pipe and sucked on the stem, his wrinkled cheeks pulling tight around the wide Slavic bones in his face. "Play Tchaikovsky," he said, smoke blooming from his mouth as he spoke.

I closed my eyes and tried to hear the opening phrase. I couldn't. All at once, exhaustion sank into me. Had I slept at all last night? I couldn't remember. I did remember exchanging hate emails with Jeremy King, playing my violin, a bizarre secret phone call to Diana—or maybe I'd dreamt all of that.

Yuri glared.

The Tchaikovsky was twenty-nine minutes long and the number of potential mistakes was probably up somewhere in the millions. I used to love it. When had that changed?

"So play it."

Yuri tossed the music onto his desk and it fluttered open to a page in the middle of the first movement. Staffs, stems, ledger lines, they looked like fractured railroad tracks, splattered with thousands of tiny black notes disfigured with flats and sharps. And then there were Yuri's markings. He used a blunt-tipped sketching pencil that made heavy metallic lines, and graphite smudges. The words, in all caps with occasional expletives, cluttered every empty space.

Something in my stomach tilted and rolled. Three pills was officially no longer enough.

"Can I use the bathroom, please?"

He rolled his eyes.

I put my violin down, grabbed my purse, and hurried off to the bathroom. Thankfully I'd brought them. I fished the pills from my purse and took one with a gulp of tap water. Yuri knew I took Inderal, just not for lessons. I flushed the toilet, washed my hands, and took a few deep breaths before heading back out.

"Should I go watch another episode of *Bachelor*, or are you playing Tchaikovsky today?" Yuri said as I took my violin and bow back out.

Apparently I'd used up my allotted thimbleful of patience for this lesson. For a brief second, I wondered what it would feel like to take my bow and whack it against that elegant ebony stand. Probably pretty good. At first, anyway. I was sick of being in trouble, no matter how hard I worked. If I hated the Tchaikovsky Violin Concerto, maybe it wasn't my fault.

But I needed Yuri. I couldn't win without him.

I put my violin on my shoulder and played.

SCARED?

The ad featured the single word, white lettering over a black-and-white photo of a girl's upturned face, her eyes large and searching, staring through me. She looked my age. It was one of hundreds of posters for Heart to Heart Adoption Services plastered on trains. I'd seen it plenty of times before.

I thought about my violin lesson. It had been two full hours of trying and failing to do exactly what Yuri was telling me, while he got more and more frustrated. He had yelled, and then, even worse, he'd given up, shrunk back into his hunched body, and turned away. Dismissed me with a defeated shrug. I'd slunk out.

I didn't want to tell Diana about the lesson. Maybe she wouldn't ask.

In less than two weeks I'd be facing Jeremy King and the Guarneri.

SCARED?

I stared at the pregnant girl in the ad. She had no idea.

When I got home there was a single email waiting for me. It was from Jeremy.

Carmen,

An ass? Wow. Bold of you.

Jeremy

P.S. I don't need luck.

Chapter 6

Jeremy King's bio was complete crap. Bios generally are (mine definitely walked the line between flowery and obnoxious), but his read like a good long swig of cherry cough syrup.

I sat in bed and read it again. And again. I stared at the photo, hating that cherubic little boy grin, then went back to the lengthy description of his fabulous career. Ego dripped from every word. I closed the dog-eared program and lay back down.

He probably hadn't written it. I knew that. I certainly hadn't written mine. But after yesterday, his pompous sneer was permanently imprinted on my brain, and I could just picture him sitting at a computer and stringing together sentences like, "His golden tone and tender touch have moved audiences across the continents to tears." I was half-surprised it didn't claim his vibrato could cure cancer.

From a business standpoint, I got it. A bio has to tell everyone who just shelled out money for tickets that they're about to hear the best violinist in the world. But that didn't make it easier to stomach.

I flopped back on my pillow and stared at the ceiling, then with just my left hand, played the opening measures of the Tchaikovsky into my mattress. My performance with the Chicago Symphony Orchestra was on Saturday. Jeremy's would be tomorrow. The concert series was supposed to get the public geared up for the competition, but I was doubtful. This is a city with six national sports teams. The average Chicagoan doesn't give a crap about a violin competition.

According to the symphony folder I'd peeked into at the CSO office last week, Jeremy would be playing the Beethoven Concerto, which meant he was probably playing the same concerto for the Guarneri too.

I tossed the program into the air, watching the pages fan and flutter to the floor. All Jeremy's bio told me was the basics. He was born and raised in London, and he was a scholarship student at the Yehudi Menuhin School of Music. After that, it read too much like my own life. He'd won the British and European equivalents of the American competitions my own bio bragged about. We'd even made our solo debuts with symphonies at the same age—nine. None of that told me what I needed to know. Neither had seeing him walk out of Symphony Center or getting those obnoxious emails.

A siren blared outside my window and then faded as it headed east toward Lake Michigan. Toward Symphony Center.

I had to hear him play.

Inderal had saved me. I hated everything about those powdery-orange hexagonal pills, starting with the bitter taste they left on the back of my tongue, but I didn't have a choice anymore. The more I used them, the more I needed to be saved.

It had started with Diana. No, that's not quite fair. It had started with the worst performance of my life.

Before Tokyo, I had never given much thought to stage fright. I had grown up onstage. Any problems I had with nerves had been worked out before the age of seven. Nerves were for the unprepared, or for the people who lacked talent and needed a scapegoat.

But then Tokyo happened. It was last spring, the last stop on my first Asian tour and I was playing my new Strad. At first, I felt nothing unusual. I stood at the edge of stage left, waiting for my cue to walk on while Diana adjusted the purple lotus blossom in my hair and picked stray threads off my silk shantung gown. She fluttered. That was what she did, how she handled her stress. But it wasn't Diana that rattled me.

The Tokyo Philharmonic was tuning on stage as the audience filtered back in from intermission. The concert was sold out, but it wasn't the audience that set me off either. Packed houses were the norm and audiences were too easily impressed to be scary.

I closed my eyes, concentrating on the adrenaline coursing through me. That thrill, that plummeting-roller-coaster feeling, always hit right before. Trying to concentrate on something, to focus my thoughts, helped. I willed my index finger steady and traced my name in cursive on the red velvet curtain, almost like leaving graffiti on a brick wall. I'd never actually held a can of spray paint, but I understood the urge. It would be nice to change all the places I'd been. The audiences would leave and forget, but there was some weird appeal in making the concert halls remember me. Too bad finger-tracing on velvet wasn't permanent.

Then I turned and looked at the musicians, and everything changed. Some were looking at their music, others were staring out into the audience, a few were whispering with each other.

But then my eyes fell on the principal second violinist. His violin rested on his knee, and his eyes bored right into me, expressionless. Why was he staring at me? What was he thinking? Suddenly, his face didn't look expressionless. It looked angry.

All around him, the throng of violinists continued their fidgeting, their whispering. What were any of them thinking? I'd never really wondered before. They had impossible-to-win chairs in one of the best symphonies in the world, but they weren't the soloist tonight or any night. Of course. They'd all played the Sibelius Concerto, probably knew my part as well as I did. They'd probably dreamed of being the soloist their whole lives. But they weren't. They were waiting to accompany me. They must hate me.

My gut twisted up. My fingers turned cold and sweaty. *They hate me.* The stage manager's earpiece crackled with static and he said something in Japanese into the micro-phone at his lips. Then he tapped my shoulder. His finger felt sharp on my bare skin, and he said, "If you please, miss," with a nod of his head. He gestured to the stage.

I didn't please. The neck of my violin felt suddenly slippery in my palm. *They want me to screw up.* Why hadn't I realized that before? I couldn't play with my hands this shaky.

A crowd had gathered behind me: backstage people,

sound technicians, extra musicians who weren't playing until the second half, and anyone else milling around who wanted to see what Carmen Bianchi, the child prodigy with the million-dollar Gibson Strad, looked like right before she went on stage, wanted to hear from the sidelines so they could go back and tell their friends, "She wasn't that great, and her nose is much bigger in person."

But I had no choice. I swallowed and charged into the open space before me. At the sound of my heels on the stage, the musicians sprang to their feet and the audience erupted with deafening applause. My knees nearly buckled. I blinked against the harshness of the stage lights and forced my feet to keep moving, nearly tripping over an electrical cord as I passed in front of the violins. *Smile*, I thought, knowing Diana was silently willing me to look the part.

At center stage, I shook the conductor's hand, then the concertmaster's. Their firm grips should have anchored me, but they squeezed too hard, and shook too vigorously. I nearly toppled over my own feet.

The noise, which had been overwhelming, suddenly died. Silence was worse. The oboist's "A" floated up from the woodwind section and I tuned, feeling every musician on stage listening, judging my ear already. I closed my eyes and swallowed, then nodded to the conductor to begin.

The opening of the Sibelius Violin Concerto is

supposed to sparkle like ice crystals. It should have been Finland at night, glittering with snow. It was the wrong concerto for this disaster. If only I was playing Brahms, I could come crashing out of the gate, fingers flying, strings snapping, then I could have hidden my nerves long enough to get control. Sibelius was too still, too transparent. On the first note, my bow skidded and bounced. My vibrato sounded too tight but I couldn't loosen it, and then I overshot the first shift.

That sour note hung in the concert hall, ringing in everyone's ears. I could feel the disappointment of every musician in the house. No, not disappointment. Satisfaction.

More skidding, more awkward bow changes, more agony followed, until my heart stopped sprinting and slowed a little, and then a little more until it reached its normal pace. Eventually, my fingers grew steadier and autopilot took over so I could hide in the back of my brain and pretend I was somewhere else. Thousands of hours of practice drove my body through the performance. I barely remembered the rest.

The postconcert hoopla was torture. The fake smiling and schmoozing dragged on and on, first with musicians, then the conductor, then with the rich patrons whose donations earned face time with whomever they wanted to meet. I was the emperor in his new clothes, and nobody would admit I had been naked. But we all knew. I'd sucked.

Finally, when I climbed into the cab to go back to the hotel, I'd put my head in Diana's lap and cried like a little girl. She hadn't said much, but took the clips out of my hair and combed through it with her fingers, letting me leak mascara all over her white skirt.

Diana had been smart. She'd waited for two weeks, until after we'd come home and the humiliation had dried. I'd spent those two weeks reading, going for daily runs with Clark, watching *America's Next Top Model* marathons. I only practiced an hour or so a day. It was nice.

"Chocolate?" Diana had asked, holding out a box of my favorites, Callebaut milk chocolate truffles. I was stretched out on the couch reading *My Name Is Asher Lev*.

"Of course." I took one and popped it into my mouth.

"Haven't you already read that?" she asked and sat down beside me, forcing me to bend my legs and make room for her.

"Yup."

I let the truffle melt in my mouth and turned the page.

"So, let's talk about Tokyo."

She was trying so hard to be casual, but the words jumped out as if she'd snapped her fingers in front of my eyes.

"Tokyo," I said.

"Yes, Tokyo."

I'd spent the last two weeks pushing it out of my

thoughts. Now that I was being forced to think about it, I had the sudden urge to throw up.

"That can't happen again," she said. Her words were slow and even. "Careers don't survive more than one of that kind of catastrophe."

"I don't know what to say," I said softly. "I don't know what happened. I just . . ."

"I know, honey." She held out the shiny gold box of truffles again, but I shook my head. "I've been thinking about a solution, and I have an idea. Yuri thinks it's a good one."

I waited. A *solution*. It hadn't even occurred to me that anyone else could fix this mess.

"We can't ignore it. It will happen again, and it doesn't matter how incredible you really are if you self-destruct onstage."

The words sounded rehearsed, and she looked straight ahead at the painting on the wall.

"Performance anxiety is a real issue for a lot of musicians," she continued. "It's an actual disorder, and there are medications available that can help you deal with it. They're called beta-blockers." She cleared her throat. "If you'd like, we could get you a prescription."

A prescription. A dozen questions descended. Would they make me jittery? Would I play as well? Were they *allowed*?

Instead I asked, "Would anybody know?"

"Of course not."

"But what would it feel like?"

"Just like it does when you're practicing. Beta-blockers don't make people better musicians. They'll just take care of the nerves. That's all."

So simple. That was all I wanted. It wasn't like an athlete taking steroids to get stronger—I already *was* the violinist I wanted to be. My mind cycled around and around. I needed this to work. I needed it to be right. But she wouldn't be suggesting it if it was wrong, if it was cheating. Yuri agreed, she had said.

I wanted her to look at me, but she was still staring at the painting.

"Did you used to take them?" I asked.

Her eyebrows lifted just a little, almost imperceptibly. I'd caught her by surprise.

"No," she said.

"Why not?"

"I didn't need them."

Of course she didn't. I should have known.

Diana had already scheduled the appointment with Dr. Wright. He came highly recommended, she said. I wasn't worried. Dry cleaners, massage therapists, violin teachers, bikini waxers—Diana thoroughly researched all her professionals.

"Describe what it feels like," he said.

Dr. Wright didn't look like a psychiatrist. He looked like a first-year med student in his big brother's lab coat. Why would a psychiatrist need a lab coat anyway, unless he was specifically trying to look more "medical"?

"Carmen?"

"Sorry?" I said.

"The performance anxiety. How does that feel?" His voiced cracked.

Like someone is squeezing my stomach and pouring liquid nitrogen on my joints, I wanted to say. "Bad," I said.

Diana cleared her throat. She sat beside me with hands clasped over her knee. Apparently one-word answers were not going to fly.

"My hands shake," I said. "My stomach hurts."

Dr. Wright nodded and wrote something down. "Do you generally sleep well?"

"Besides the violin nerves, she's a normal, happy, teenage girl," Diana said.

Dr. Wright's timid gaze went from me to Diana to me again. He looked like he was trying to decide whether to ask me the sleep question again, or if he should just give Diana his lunch money.

"What she needs is a prescription for beta-blockers," Diana continued. "Her nerves are a pretty typical response for a soloist who's facing the kind of intense pressure that she's under. There's a lot riding on each performance—contracts, competitions, recordings, you know . . ." Her voice trailed off and she put a protective hand on my back and leaned forward in her chair. "Violin demands a lot from her, but she is one of the best in the world."

That was the clincher. Dr. Wright looked down at his desk and reached for a pen and prescription pad. He clearly didn't want to be the man standing in the way of me becoming the best violinist in the world. Or maybe he just wanted to get rid of us.

Five minutes later we were back in the safety of the Diana's Lexus listening to *Aida*, with a prescription for Inderal tucked into the zipper pocket of Diana's snakeskin clutch.

"Are you all right?" she asked.

I nodded, but didn't look at her, didn't say anything, just kept picking at the callous on the tip of my index finger.

"I know what you're worried about," she said, "but nobody else is going to know. You don't have to tell anyone. This is between you, me, and Yuri. Frankly, it isn't anyone else's business."

I nodded. Shame. Finally. It felt like rotten milk curdling in my stomach. I had spent all morning trying not to think anything, but there it was. *You, me, and Yuri.*

What about Clark? If it was really okay, he would know too. But obviously it wasn't really okay.

Diana hadn't lied about what it would be like. She just hadn't really known.

The chalky little pills looked more like vitamin C than anything else. I transferred them into a nondescript wooden pillbox and put them in the rosin pocket of my case. They looked completely innocent.

"If anyone asks," Diana said, "tell them they're for cramps."

Nobody asked. In the beginning, they worked miracles. An hour after my very first pill, I walked onstage for a performance with the Montreal Symphony with steady hands, in complete control of every movement. But by November, I needed two pills for the same steady hands. And then three. And then not just for performances, but for lessons too. I could justify that, though. Lessons are a type of performance, aren't they? Yuri's temper didn't make it easy either. I needed to be calm to get through each lesson and learn what had to be learned.

Dr. Wright said that didn't make sense. At the follow-up appointment, he said Inderal isn't *physically* addictive like that. If I felt like I needed more and more, he said, that's a *psychological* addiction, and I should just trust that the dosage he'd given me was adequate.

I left confused—had my psychiatrist just told me I was crazy? It didn't matter. *I* knew I needed at least three pills per performance. For now.

I tried not to think about it, and when I did, I told myself it was worth it. I just had to remember Tokyo and that stomach-wrenching stage fright to know it was. With Inderal, I never had to feel like that again.

Now when I was onstage, I didn't feel much of anything.

Chapter 7

leaned against the wall, a cold concrete slab in a basement hallway, and examined my ticket. *Series: Virtuosos of Tomorrow, Location: Gallery, Seat: Box B.* I'd lucked out. The woman at the will-call window had recognized me and hooked me up with the best seat in the house. I rubbed the perforated edge against my thumb and listened for any noise above the buzz of the fluorescent panels. Nothing.

My watch read 8:52. Intermission would be over in eight minutes, but it wasn't time to go up to my seat yet. The timing had to be perfect. At 8:56 I would start my climb up the elegant rotunda staircase, which would still be packed but thinning quickly. People would be hurrying into the auditorium from last-minute concession-stand trips and from the bathrooms. If I could keep my head down through six floors of spiral staircase, I might not be recognized. I needed to reach the sixth floor arcade by the time the house lights dimmed, so I'd have only a few seconds to get to the doors before the ushers closed them.

The light panel was unnaturally bright. I stared at the stairwell door and tried to tune out the fluorescent buzz overhead, which seemed to be getting louder. I wondered if Jeremy was nervous right now. He didn't seem like the type. He was probably doing his hair, trying to muss it up just right so it looked convincingly tousled. Or flirting with somebody. There were a handful of women in the symphony young enough for him to be making an idiot of himself with.

Lying to my mom had been way too easy. It was sad, really. Not the lying part, but that I was seventeen and she had no reason to doubt me when I said I was going to bed at seven on a Friday night.

I'd told her with a toothbrush in my mouth. She was holding a tube of magenta lipstick, twisted up and ready to apply. Her hair was pulled up into a sleek French twist and she wore a jade-green silk dress. A gold scarf floated around her shoulders like a sinking halo. She looked beautiful.

"I'm going to bed early," I'd said.

"Good." Her hand expertly guided the tube of lipstick over her lips and then she pressed them together. "We can't have you running out of steam tomorrow night." And then as an afterthought, "Do you want one of my sleeping pills?"

I took the toothbrush out of my mouth. "No. I'm exhausted."

"All right," she said. "Clark and I are leaving for the art show at eight. I don't think we'll be back until late, but we'll be quiet when we come in."

At 8:05 her car pulled away from the house, and by 8:10 I had replaced my pajama pants and tank top with a little black dress and heels. The dress was one I hardly ever wore, since it was too short to perform in. As an afterthought, I twisted my hair up like Diana's. The effect was not the same. Mine was too curly to be sophisticated, but what did it matter? Nobody was going to see me tonight.

I stared at myself in the mirror. What was I doing? Deliberately ignoring the part of my brain that was smart enough to ask questions, I applied a layer of red lipstick and turned off the bathroom light. Bravery was what I needed, not rational thinking. I was once again attempting espionage, and after the colossal failure at Rhapsody, that took guts. And insanity. I'd buttoned my red wool peacoat and headed out the door.

The peacoat was folded over my arm now, and I had nothing to do but listen to buzzing fluorescent lights and think of reasons I should be at home in bed. There was the sleep thing (I really did need a good night's sleep before a performance), and then there was the possibility that he was as good as everyone said and I'd be too worried to sleep and have to down a whole fistful of Inderal to get myself onstage tomorrow night.

I checked my watch again. 8:56. Time to go.

The lights dimmed as I stepped into the empty box, and all the typical auditorium noises—the talking, the coughing, the crinkling wrappers—died with them. Darkness forced every eye to the lit stage. I slid into the chair and ran a hand over the lush fabric, then pulled the edge of the velvet curtain closer.

The concertmaster rose and I examined my angle while the orchestra tuned. I could see over the cellists' shoulders and, if I leaned forward, almost read the notes off the last stand of music.

The concertmaster returned to his seat and silence settled again in the hall.

I heard Jeremy before I saw him. First came the tap and echo of men's dress shoes on wood, and then his blond head appeared, bobbing through the field of violin bows on stage right. Again, his height surprised me. He towered over the other musicians. The conductor followed him, taking two steps for every one of Jeremy's, looking like a little brother tagging along. They reached center stage, and Jeremy came around front of the podium taking a reluctant bow. His well-cut tux looked intentionally rumpled, like the jacket had been rolled up in a ball and then pressed. His hair fell over his forehead and into his eyes, and the thin line of his mouth fell flat. I couldn't label that expression. It wasn't boredom and it wasn't disdain and it wasn't mocking, but it was something that made me consider all three of those as possibilities.

Diana mandated a smile from me when I walked out on stage. Not just any smile, but a genuine, confident-but-not-cocky, happy-but-not-hyper, smile. Something for the audience to relate to. It was the kind of thing you had to practice in front of a mirror. Clearly Jeremy didn't know what he looked like right now, that was a mistake. He had everyone squirming with that sullen look.

Stage presence, according to Diana, is *not* an art. Arts have loose rules, no set right and wrong, but stage presence is much more calculated than that. It is a science, a science with formulas that had been drilled into my head—but Jeremy didn't seem to know any of them.

The conductor reached out his hand, and Jeremy looked almost surprised by it. He paused, then shook it, then tuned his violin with a few careless strokes and plucks. When he turned to face the audience, the silence turned ugly. His face was grim. People looked in their laps and fidgeted. I fought the urge to do the same. He wasn't just cranky, he was *glaring*. And then, at the moment the awkwardness became absolutely unbearable, his face broke into a huge grin. Laughter rippled through the crowd and relief warmed the air. A collective sigh rose from the audience, as if they were all in on some hilarious joke.

I looked around. Everyone was smiling stupidly and readjusting themselves in their seats, but I couldn't do it. I didn't feel like cooperating with him. Whatever trick he'd just pulled felt cheap and tacky. Very un-Beethoven. Could he not just play the music?

Still grinning out at us, Jeremy raised his eyebrows and waited for our attention again. The fidgeting and the rustling melted away, and he had it. He closed his eyes, soaking up the anticipation of the crowd for one more second, and then he did the unthinkable. He flicked his wrist and tossed his violin into the air. It spiraled upward like a fish yanked out of the water, twisting up and rotating toward his body at the same time. I gasped. We all gasped and watched it miraculously land on his shoulder where his other hand was waiting to anchor it. This time the laughter was more than a ripple. It was a wave, surging from front to back and over the entire concert hall.

I clenched my jaw and stifled the urge to cup my hands

around my mouth and boo. Instead, I started working on a list of adjectives I hoped would make the concert review: ridiculous, juvenile, insulting, pathetic . . .

The Beethoven Violin Concerto is one of the noblest pieces of music in the violin repertoire, and Jeremy had just opened the concert with all the dignity of a circus seal balancing a ball on his nose. Somewhere, six feet deep in the Rhineland soil, Beethoven was rolling over and pounding his fists in agony.

Play already, I willed him.

Jeremy gazed out at us, and I realized my mistake. Box B was too exposed. Sitting alone made it worse. I'd been too worried about being spotted by people in the audience, but now that I was removed from them, I saw the crowd would have at least hidden me. I slouched, hoping the box was dark enough and slid the chair into the curtain's shadow.

Finally, Jeremy nodded to the conductor.

The orchestra began the exposition, and Jeremy's face changed. The grin disappeared. His gaze fixed itself to the back of the hall, as if he was staring across a misty field.

I looked down. The faces below me glowed as the stage lights glanced off their profiles. They were in love, and he hadn't played a single note.

Did audiences look at me that way? I had no idea. I wanted them to. Except I wanted them to love me for my music, not for gimmicks and drama. But I *did* want people to stare up at me like that, for anticipation to push them to the edges of their chairs.

Maybe I had been performing all wrong.

When I was onstage, the audience didn't exist. It was safer to think of them as faceless silhouettes in one big anonymous mass, or better yet, not to think of them at all. As Yuri said, "Audience is bunch of idiots." He'd then pull his face into a sour pucker to accentuate just how much their pea-size brains offended him. "What do they know? You play for composer. Music is *his*."

Diana suggested an alternative to idiots and dead people. "Play for yourself," she advised. "This is your time. When you're out there onstage, it has to be about you." Then, in a slightly less idealistic tone she added, "But for heaven's sake, as your manager, I'm telling you to smile while you're out there. Nobody wants to be stared down by a surly teenager."

I wanted to protest. I was a musician, not an actress. Smiling on command made me feel like a pageant contestant, and I wasn't vying for Miss Illinois. What next, Vaseline-ing my teeth and taping my cleavage? (According to Heidi, they really did that in pageants.) But sometimes with Diana it was just easier to nod.

Jeremy lifted his bow to play. I held my breath, and without thinking, started to pray silently: *Please God, let me hear something bad. Not a mistake, but a deeper, fundamental flaw. Tight vibrato would be perfect.* But the realization that God probably didn't curse people on request, especially for quasi-believers like myself, kept me from asking for anything else. I didn't even finish it off with an *amen.* For all I knew, Jeremy was praying right now too, in which case his request would undoubtedly outrank mine. I didn't know what religion he was, but if he was even remotely devout, he had me beat.

Jeremy's bow glided across the string and the opening notes washed over me. That tone. It made me stop praying for ugliness. It made me think of sweetness, of sunshine and vanilla. It made every worrying thought slip from my mind as it surrounded me.

We all felt the pull. The notes flew out of his instrument and over us, and it was as if we were being hypnotized. He was casting a spell, but it was with more than just music. The enchantment was the story, and with every phrase he added another layer, another character, weaving us into the piece as he crossed back and forth over the strings, until we weren't sure where we ended and the music began.

I couldn't look away. He was stunning. The violin sat high on his shoulder, and looked impossibly small in his hands. He maneuvered around like it was simple, like it was nothing. The arrogance in his face was gone, and what was left was . . . calm? How was that possible? Eyes closed, he looked like he was *inside* the music.

It was almost painful to stop staring, but I had to. The sound was too much. It just couldn't be that perfect. Captivating, yes, but not flawless. I closed my eyes and listened. I would settle for the tiniest crack.

But there wasn't one. Everything was shiny and perfect.

Sadness found me in the second movement. Jealousy and frustration would have made more sense, but those required fire and there was nothing but a cold ache behind my ribs. It was too beautiful, but I couldn't stop listening. I couldn't even hate him anymore.

The plan was to slip out just before the end, but I hadn't realized I would feel like this. I didn't want to leave. I didn't even think I could stand. And at this point, what did it matter anyway? I needed to hear it all. He pounded through the final notes, dragging me along with him. I felt like I was being trampled by a galloping horse. ·

Below me, the audience couldn't wait for silence. Applause exploded the moment his bow left the string, with the entire crowd jumping to their feet, clapping, shouting *"Bravo!"* I was too weak to do anything but let the chaos explode around me.

From the safety of my perch I watched his face change, the personality seep slowly back in. At first he just looked happy and so energized, bowing and grinning and waving as he walked on and off stage again and again for his curtain calls. But then happy became flippant and flippant became narcissistic as he turned a slow circle at center stage, his arms up in the air as if trying to suck in all the adoration.

I could feel the disgust creeping back into my stomach. The music had temporarily frozen it, but it was still there and thawing quickly. He flashed the conductor that arrogant smile, and tossed his head to bounce those ridiculous bangs out of his face. What an idiot.

For his final curtain call, Jeremy swaggered back out onto the stage even slower than before and held up his hands to the audience in what looked like a stop-don't-shoot move. He was surrendering. We won. He'd play an encore. Then he reached up to the conductor, put his hand on his shoulder, and leaned over to whisper something in his ear. Whatever he said prompted a surprised look from the conductor, who offered a quick word to the section leaders. A flurry of page flipping followed as every musician onstage rifled through their folders.

"It seems," the conductor said as he turned to face us, "the young maestro has had a change of heart concerning his encore. Lucky for him, we are performing this piece next week and happen to have the music handy to oblige." He forced a laugh, short and shallow. Maybe

I wasn't the only one getting irked by the ego.

Jeremy didn't notice, or ignored it. The look on his face said the possibility of it not working out hadn't occurred to him.

The conductor sniffed and raised his eyebrows at Jeremy, who took that as his cue to finally speak.

"I guess I'm feeling dramatic tonight," he said. The audience laughed, more at the accent than what he said. What was it that made British English so charming?

"So dramatic," he continued, "I'd like to play something from my favorite opera. This is Pablo de Sarasate's take on a little Bizet opera you might be familiar with." He paused long enough to put his violin under his chin, angle his jaw straight at Box B, and stare right into my eyes.

My stomach fell and fell and fell.

"*Carmen Fantasy*," he announced, and lifted his bow.

For the first time since the Beethoven had ended he wasn't smiling. His face held all the aggression of a matador staring into the eyes of a bull. He might as well have been waving a red flag at me as the cellos began playing the sultry gypsy theme.

I wanted to put my head in my hands and die, but I couldn't break away from his stare. Eventually, he looked away, at his violin, and dove into the music without looking back.

He played *Carmen* perfectly. I think. I only half heard

him. Instead, my brain went over the rocky ledge of trauma and panic, where I held on by my fingernails. *Dear God, please let the earth crack open, suck me in, and swallow me whole.*

Chapter 8

ran my fingers over the embossed letters. JEREMY KING. The exaggerated italics reminded me of his accent. Pretentious. Lilting to the point of nearly falling over. I fought the urge to tear the placard off the dressing room door and stuff it into my jacket pocket. It would need to be taken down soon anyway. This was supposed to be my dressing room tomorrow night, which meant there was an identical card with *Carmen Bianchi* in the same flowery script just waiting to go up. I would be doing them a favor, and besides, it was nice to think of him so easily removed and replaced.

I smoothed the lap wrinkles from my dress. I'd been

thinking about blending in with the other cocktail dresses when I'd put this little black dress on, but now I felt too, too . . . glammed up. The last thing I wanted was for Jeremy to think I was trying to make that kind of impression on him. Of course, going backstage to talk to him had not been part the plan before he'd forced me into it. Maybe I was overthinking things.

I lifted my hand, not sure whether I was going to rip off the card or knock. I'd have already left if it weren't for Yuri's voice in my head. It was there from time to time, usually nagging and always out of context. "Stop being baby," was the advice I was currently ruminating on.

And now—standing outside of Jeremy's dressing room, holding my red coat, chewing my lower lip raw, and staring at the *Jeremy King* card—I knew the advice applied. Being a baby had gotten me into this mess, and if I took off now, he'd think I was too scared to meet him. The encore was a dare.

I stopped thinking and knocked.

I only had a few seconds to regret it before the door swung open. There stood Jeremy King, one hand on the knob, the other holding a can of Dr Pepper up to his mouth. His tuxedo shirt was open at the neck, his jacket and bow tie were behind him, strewn over the armchair.

It took me a moment to find words. Offstage and up close, he was a magnified version of what he'd been from the audience—taller, and sharper featured, with an angular jaw and blue eyes.

He raised his eyebrows, probably because I was just standing there like a mute idiot. I extended my hand. "Carmen Bianchi."

"I know." He shook it.

His hand was huge. It seemed unfair. Violin would be so much easier with hands like that.

"I'm surprised," he said and stepped back, motioning for me to come in. "I was starting to think you didn't want to meet me." The signature grin was gone, and his tone was guarded.

I glanced around the dressing room. It was the same as last time I'd seen it, spacious and decorated with lavish-but-dated furniture: a worn velvet couch, a baby grand piano, lightbulb-bordered mirrors, and generic paintings of the Hudson River and the Chicago skyline. His violin was already packed up, and a dress bag rested beside it on the couch.

I looked around the room again, this time for a parent or a manager or a teacher. He was alone.

"Looking for someone?"

"No. I just assumed you'd have an entourage back here."

"No entourage."

"You always tour alone?"

He shrugged. "My dad couldn't be off work for that long, and my mom stays home with my brother."

I nodded, processing this information. I imagined being in London without Diana, staying in a hotel by myself, eating alone, performing without anybody waiting for me backstage. It would either be incredible or sad. Maybe both.

I had been quiet too long. Jeremy was staring at me, waiting for me to speak.

"I want to apologize for the other day, at the café," I stammered.

"Don't," he said. "I'm the one who should apologize. The salute was a bit much."

"But I should have said hi. I just wasn't expecting to see you. I was caught by surprise."

It was a lie, but my only option if I didn't want him to think I was an obsessed stalker. There was just no way I could admit to spying and come off sounding sane. Besides, the encounter *could* have been accidental.

He raised an eyebrow. "Surprise? I doubt it."

"Excuse me?"

He squinted, probably trying to decide just how awkward he was willing to make this. "I think you were waiting for me."

My brain stalled. Not believing me, or at least not pretending to, had not been part of the plan. "That's a little pretentious, don't you think?" I managed. "Why would I be spying on you?"

"Spying? *I* never said spying," he said. "I thought you were waiting to meet me and then chickened out. Spying. . . . Wow. Don't you think that's a little, I don't know, juvenile?"

This was not going well. "I said I *wasn't* spying."

"Sure." He nodded and gave me a look that said the opposite.

Crap. I had overestimated his social skills. He was a complete jackass. "Chickened out?" I repeated, angry now. "No offense, but you're not exactly a rock star. If I'd wanted to meet you, I would have done that."

He rolled his eyes. "Like you did tonight," he said.

"Yes. Exactly."

"But that's not true. You came to introduce yourself because I practically forced you into it with the encore. Did you enjoy it, by the way?"

I stared at him, wishing I hadn't already apologized. I wasn't sorry for anything. I'd assumed the encore was his way of saying, *Hey loser—think I don't see you up there?* It hadn't occurred to me that he was goading me into coming backstage just for a confrontation. If that was the case, I'd done exactly what he'd bullied me into doing.

He grinned, obviously proud of himself, like it was nothing short of genius to taunt me with music from the opera I was named after. "I almost didn't recognize you without the Medusa hair you have on all your CD covers, but once I was sure it was you, I couldn't help myself."

I'd forgotten that my hair was up. I reached for the clip and yanked it out, then spun around to leave.

"Hey, simmer down," he said as he reached out and gripped my upper arm with his hand, stopping me mid-spin. Clearly, he thought he owned the world and everybody in it.

It hurt. Not his grip, but the accusation that I was overreacting. He thought I was being dramatic, getting all riled up for no reason, that *I* was socially inept, when he was the one being a complete jerk.

I glared at him, feeling stupid even as I was doing it. His smile was different now. Not the grin I'd seen over and over, but something closer to sincere. If he was capable of that.

"I've offended you," he said. His voice had lost a shade or two of the obnoxiousness along with the smirk, but there was still an irking confidence. "I didn't mean to. Let me buy you dinner as an apology."

I looked down at his hand, still holding my arm. He let go.

"Actually, I need to get home. I'm performing tomorrow night."

"Oh, right." He picked up a gray sweater from off the sofa. "We'll eat quickly then."

He pulled the sweater over his head and turned off the lights while I wondered what was going on and where my spine had disappeared to. In the dark I felt his hand on my arm again, this time turning me toward the door and pushing me out.

"What are you doing?" Jeremy asked.

"Eating."

"No, I mean why are you doing that to your pizza?"

I looked down at my slice of thin-crust. I'd folded it down the middle, crust-side out.

"Because it tastes better this way."

We sat side by side in a circle of yellow lamplight, a cold park bench beneath us, an open pizza box between us. I'd kicked off my heels and tucked my feet underneath me to keep them warm. Further down the path, another yellow circle lit an empty bench, and then another one and another one, in a glowing chain of empty yellow spotlights throughout Millennium Park.

"I doubt it," he said.

"Trust me. It makes it a tasty pocket of pizza goodness."

"I don't think doing origami with my pizza is going to change the taste."

"But my way you don't get your hands dirty."

He shrugged. "That at least makes sense." He chewed his own piece thoughtfully then asked, "Isn't Chicago pizza supposed to be deep-dish?"

"That's just what we tell the tourists. Plenty of decent thin-crust here too."

Jeremy nodded, took another bite. Since we'd left Symphony Center, he'd been almost normal. It had been minutes since I remembered what a jerk he was. "Just fold it and see," I said.

"So American," he mumbled, disgust in his voice as he licked pizza sauce off his fingers.

"What's that supposed to mean?"

"Assuming there's only one way to do something, like eating pizza, and insisting everyone else do it your way."

Oh yeah, I did hate him.

"That's so British," I countered.

"What is?"

"Making sweeping generalizations about Americans because that makes you feel better about having a national inferiority complex the size of the Atlantic Ocean. I was just trying to be helpful, but if folded pizza threatens your sense of patriotism, you probably shouldn't do it."

He squinted at me. "Sheesh. American and crabby. Fine, I'll fold the pizza." He made a little ceremony of folding it exactly down the center and taking a bite. "Mmm," he said. "Now that *is* a tasty pocket of pizza goodness."

"I'll ignore the sarcasm and accept that as a victory."

"Because everything is a contest?"

I didn't answer. Of course it was.

The pizza had been my suggestion. Jeremy had requested authentic Chicago, so we'd hit Marco's Italian, a hole-in-the-wall take-out window on Wabash around the corner from Symphony Center, and then headed across the street to Millennium Park. I was happy with the choice. There was something nice about the mix of dissimilar sensations—shivering on a cement bench, eating hot, salty pizza, and smelling lilac blossoms.

I glanced over at Jeremy. His thick blond bangs covered his eyes, soaking up the yellow lamplight.

"So you're here by yourself until the Guarneri?" I asked.

"Yeah."

"Doing what?"

"Practicing. Sightseeing. Whatever."

I nodded. His voice still didn't tell me whether he was happy with that or not. Again, I imagined myself in a strange city by myself for a few weeks, totally dependent on public transport, restaurants, hotel laundry.

"Where are you staying?"

"The Drake. Do you know it?"

"Sure." At least he wasn't roughing it. The Drake Hotel was the only place the Glenns would stay when they were in Chicago, not that it was ever just to visit me. Traditional, expensive, uppity—the same words I could use to describe them, actually. It was old but elegant, sitting on the far north edge of the Magnificent Mile with views of Lake Michigan and the high-end fashion district. Jeremy was living the good life.

"So, what am I looking at?" he asked. He gestured to the stone slab in front of us, engraved with a long list of names.

"The park's founders."

"Oprah Winfrey? Really? Bill and Hillary Clinton?"

"Uh, yeah." I put my slice down, half eaten. "My grandparents are up there too. Thomas and Dorothy Glenn. Second column."

"Wow," he said, then glanced at me. "So you're Chicago royalty."

"Not really. And they're New Yorkers actually, but they donate to a few projects here in Chicago too."

"Like you."

"What?"

"Like you."

"I heard you the first time," I said. "I just didn't understand what you meant by it."

"I thought I'd read they bought your Strad. Isn't that true?"

It was true, but it wasn't any of his business, and I wasn't sure where he'd read about it.

"They did," I said.

"Lucky girl."

"That's an interesting choice of words."

"Oh, right. Lucky woman. Sorry."

"No," I said. "Lucky. There's an implication there."

"As the one who was supposedly doing the implicating, should I know what you're talking about?" He picked up the last slice of pizza—*my* half-eaten slice, the one I'd just put down—and took a bite.

"I think you do. Lucky means undeserved."

"It doesn't have to." He stifled a grin. Apparently, he found my temper hilarious.

"But it did when you said it," I said. The realization that I was fighting an unwinnable argument made me mad. Mad enough to push him off the bench. Instead, I grabbed my piece of pizza out of his hand and chewed off an enormous bite. "And I wasn't done with this."

He stared at me, eyes wide.

I kept chewing and turned back to glare at the monument. Lots of musicians have instruments purchased for them by wealthy patrons. My patrons just happened to be related.

It was hard to tell exactly when I started feeling like an idiot, but it was definitely sometime after I swallowed that chewed lump of pizza and before he started laughing. I refused to look at him.

"Shut up," I said, but it lost impact because I was laughing too.

"You have one crazy Dr. Jekyll inside of you," he said.

"No, Dr. Jekyll is the nice one. Mr. Hyde is the maniac."

He squinted, rubbing his palm over his jaw and the faintest shade of stubble there. "Are you sure?"

"Yes."

"I don't know whether you're right or wrong, but at this point, I'm scared to question you," he said.

"Good. And just so you know, I'm not one of those kids who've had every opportunity purchased for them. My grandparents bought the violin, but that's it. Up until last year, I was just an embarrassing reminder of their son's playboy years." I shrugged. Why was I telling him this?

He sat quietly, looking down at the pavement.

"As far as they're concerned," I added, "I didn't even exist until I was famous."

He nodded and said softly, "It's a weird kind of fame though, isn't it?" He reached down and followed a crack in the cement with his index finger. "You're a god to two percent of the population, and a nobody to everyone else.

At least your grandparents are part of the two percent. My dad's parents aren't. They're still annoyed at my mum and dad for letting me skip Christmas for a concert tour last year. And my dad still hasn't given up the dream of seeing me go to medical school."

It seemed hard to believe that anyone who played the violin like Jeremy could come from an unartistic family. "Your mom," I said, "is she a musician?"

"Music lover. Not quite the same thing."

"True," I said, thinking of Clark. He was a music lover by marriage. His efforts—coming to my concerts, putting up with the constant shoptalk, just existing in the energy vacuum of my career—were kind of sweet, especially considering he was totally tone-deaf. "Somebody has to buy tickets," I said, thinking of the full house Jeremy had just performed in front of.

"You think they're all actually music lovers?"

"In the audience?" I said. "Why else would they be there?"

He shrugged. "That's what I can't figure out. Why come if you don't love it?"

"But what makes you think they don't love it?"

"I don't know. I just don't see how nonmusicians can even understand enough about the music to enjoy it."

I had no answer. The onstage persona of Jeremy King was starting to make sense. He didn't think they were even there to hear him. The tricks and bravado had been tactical, like I'd thought, but covering something sad. I didn't think about my audience when I was onstage, but I at least assumed they were listening to me.

"I love it because I can create it," he said. "Don't you find having to sit and listen to anyone else play frustrating?"

"I guess a little." I had tonight. Not that I could tell him that. He'd think I was intimidated.

"Of that two percent who know who we are," he continued. "I'd guess only half really love the music we make."

"So your mom, is she part of that one percent?"

"Yeah." He paused. "And yours?"

The question surprised me. I hadn't really thought about it. My career was her entire life, how could I not know? "I guess. But she's a musician. Or was."

"I know," he said. "I've heard of her."

I had the bizarre urge to tell him about Diana, how the stunted opera career fed her impossibly high expectations. He would have understood. But I couldn't. It felt like betrayal. Talking about the Glenns was safer.

"My grandparents are part of the two percent, I guess, but not the half that actually enjoy music," I said. "I think they like to pretend. It's what people in their social circle do, dress up in Gucci and sprinkle money on the lowly artists. Who knows though, when I win the Guarneri, maybe they'll hook me up with a trust fund."

He snorted and leaned over, elbows on knees, fingers laced. His face looked hard, and I knew I'd said something wrong. I shouldn't have mentioned the Guarneri.

"You sound confident," he said.

"I am."

"Hmmm," he said and glanced back at me, over his shoulder. He didn't believe me. He knew I was scared. I looked away.

"Sorry," he said, and shook his head. "I have a hard time letting my competitive side drop."

"I understand."

I did understand. One minute I wanted to pick his brain and tell him everything I was thinking, and the next minute I wanted slam his hand in a door.

We sat, not talking, listening to the cicadas chirp, interrupted by the occasional honk from down the path, where the park met Lake Shore Drive.

"You know what I love about performing?" he asked. His tone had relaxed again.

"The applause," I joked.

He ignored me. "I love the almost-done. You know, when you're far enough along and you've got the right momentum and you know you aren't going to screw it up, but you're still out there, still flying."

I closed my eyes and leaned into the back of the bench. It hadn't felt like flying in a long time.

"Yeah," I said. Deep in my stomach, I felt the sadness again.

I had been wrong about Jeremy understanding me. Nobody could. He came close, closer than anyone else, but then Inderal ruined it. It separated my type of genius from his type of genius.

"You're beautiful," he said.

I opened my eyes.

Jeremy's hair still hung in his eyes and the lamplight washed over his features, casting pointy shadows from his chin and nose.

I needed a response. I couldn't think.

"What time is it?" I asked.

He blinked. It was the wrong thing to say.

"The time," he said, and leaned back so he could reach into his pocket for his cell phone, "is 1:48."

"Oh, crap." I reached down and fumbled for my heels. I had to get home.

"Past your bedtime?"

"Kind of," I said, suddenly aware that I was talking to someone who was allowed to cross continents unsupervised. He would think I was a complete baby if I told him I had snuck out. "I'm performing tomorrow night. I should be asleep right now."

He nodded, stood up, and took a step out of the lamplight. "You're one of those people who freaks out if their pre-performance rituals aren't just right, aren't you?" I couldn't see his face anymore, but scorn had entered his voice. "You seem uptight like that," he added, more to himself than to me.

My stomach twisted over on itself. He'd said I was beautiful. And then I'd said the wrong thing, and now I didn't know what was going on, except that it felt like I'd ruined something.

"I wouldn't call a good night's sleep a ritual," I stammered. "It's just common sense. I'm hardly demanding all the brown M&M's be removed from the premises."

"What are you talking about?"

Why did he sound so mean? "Van Halen. It was written into all his contracts. Someone had to go through bowls of M&M's for his dressing room and remove all the brown ones." That was Clark's one area of musical expertise, eighties heavy metal. He had been proud to fill my brain with hard-rock trivia, and I'd been happy to let him because it bugged Diana.

"Whatever." Jeremy shrugged, unimpressed.

I stood up. He didn't offer me a hand. Not that I'd have taken it.

We started down the snaking path back to Lake Shore Drive in silence.

"This is weird," he said finally.

I said nothing. It *was* weird. Wandering around in a

freezing cold park after midnight, that was weird. Hanging out with a guy, sadly that was weird too, not to mention that he was my nemesis, my main competition, the one person who could stand in the way of everything I'd always wanted. Being told I was beautiful, the weirdest of all. Add to that: Jeremy's completely manic behavior, my lying and sneaking out, and then spending half the night before an important performance freezing to death in Millennium Park, and the big ball of weirdness was complete.

"I'm having a hard time knowing whether or not to hate you," he said.

"That was honest. At least the feeling is mutual," I said.

"I want to be nice, but then I remember who you are, and I can't," he continued. "So I turn into a jerk, but then you make that difficult."

"Hmmm," I said, because I didn't know what else there was.

He snorted. "It would be more convenient if you weren't so . . ."

Finish! If I weren't so . . . But he didn't.

Instead he said, "Are you nervous?"

"For tomorrow? Not really." That was the medicated truth.

"No, I mean for the Guarneri."

"Yeah," I said, before I could stop myself. So much for my poker face.

But my Guarneri dread was hard to lie about. It wasn't regular performance fear, the stuff that Inderal could take care of. It wasn't about performing at all. It was about what happened after.

"Me too," he said. His voice was quiet but steady.

"I didn't think you were the nervous type," I said. "And according to your bio, you don't ever lose."

"According to yours, neither do you."

Losing. I'd been working too hard at keeping the thought from wriggling up to the surface. Now couldn't possibly be the best moment for letting it through. Making a *what-if-I-lose* plan with Jeremy King was nothing less than self-sabotage.

We had reached Lake Shore Drive without me noticing. Jeremy lifted his hand, and a taxi pulled up beside us.

He turned and gave me a rueful look. He was embarrassed. The realization mostly confused me. "Split a cab?" he asked and opened the door for me.

I nodded, climbed in and slid over. He sat down beside me. I rattled off my address, and the cab pulled away from the curb.

"We probably shouldn't be friends, you know," he said, but not convincingly. He didn't seem to notice that our legs were touching.

"Probably not. I mean, right now we're just rude to each other off and on, but in two weeks, we'll hate each other. Or at least one of us will."

"I don't think I'll hate you," he said.

"That's because you think you'll win."

"No." He paused. "I mean, yes. I think I'll win. But even if I don't win, I don't think I *could* hate you."

I felt strange. Angry first—why was he so sure he could win?—then light-headed, almost giddy. Saying he couldn't hate me, was that almost saying he liked me? And when had I stopped hating him and started . . . not hating him?

The cab swerved left suddenly and the driver swore, jarring my brain back into the moment. I looked at Jeremy. He was staring out the window. Losing the Guarneri to him would suck. A whole herd of lovesick butterflies in my stomach wouldn't change that. An encore dedication, a midnight walk in the park, being told I was beautiful— those added up to a big fat nothing beside everything that I'd been working for. If he beat me I would hate him. And probably myself too.

Jeremy looked up and smiled. I smiled back. He was either a better person, or a liar. Or he really liked me, but that seemed less plausible. He didn't even know me.

We rode in silence. Understanding had drained the pressure: we mutually liked and hated each other. Nothing could be done about it. One of us would win, the loser's life would be over, and no matter what he was trying to convince himself of, forgiveness would be impossible.

Then he lifted his arm and draped it around my shoulders and I found myself falling into the curve of his body, the gray wool of his sweater prickly against my neck and face. He smelled like cinnamon gum and aftershave. I hoped he couldn't feel my heart racing.

"So, we've got less than two weeks. Are you going to show me around Chicago?" he asked.

Diana's face appeared in my mind. She had already scheduled every minute of the next two weeks for me. I imagined telling her I was going to waste a day riding the Ferris wheel at Navy Pier and taking pictures from the top of the Sears Tower with Jeremy King. She wouldn't freak out. She was too dignified for freaking out. She'd just say no.

"Um, maybe," I stalled.

"Maybe you will, or maybe you'll come up with a good excuse not to?"

"Truthfully, my mom has me on a short leash."

"Because the Guarneri is in two weeks."

"Well . . . no, it's more constant than that."

"Just how short is the leash?" he asked.

I paused. Why lie? "She thinks I've been asleep since seven."

"That's short."

"Yes, it is."

"So she would definitely freak if she found out you were playing with the enemy," he said.

I nodded, thinking how badly I wanted to reach out and sweep his hair out of his eyes.

"Give me your phone," he said. I pulled it from my coat pocket and handed it over, watching him as he thumb-typed into it, wondering what I was doing.

"Now you've got my mobile number," he said. "I'm calling it, so your number is in my phone too."

"'Mobile,'" I said, and laughed. "So British."

His dial tone sounded just once from his pocket before he closed my phone.

"Yes, good observation. I'm still British. I'll probably continue to be that way." He handed my phone back to me and his hand held onto mine for just a second, then let go. "Call me if you want to do something."

"It's not if I *want*. It's if I *can*."

He stared at me. "You're almost eighteen, Carmen," he said. "What's the difference?"

I wanted to defend myself, but nothing came. He was staring at me, waiting for me to say I'd call. I felt the taxi slow and pull over, but I kept my eyes on his face.

"Is that your house?" He pointed out the window behind me.

I turned and as I did my stomach fell. The brownstone was glowing like a firefly against the black night. My room. Diana and Clark's room. The front room. The porch. Every light was on.

"Oh, no," I whispered and reached for the door handle.

"Wait," he said, putting his hand on my arm, and before I had time to realize what was happening, he leaned forward and kissed me. I closed my eyes and felt his other hand cradle my head against the surprising pressure of his lips. Then it was over. He pulled back.

My heart pounded. I didn't want to open my eyes, didn't want to have to get out of the cab and step back into my life. But Jeremy was wrong—there is a huge difference between doing what you want to do and doing what you have to do.

"Good night," I whispered, my voice lost somewhere in my chest. I tottered dizzily from the car, nearly tipping over on my heels. I stared up. The black night, white stars, and yellow house lights glimmered like fractured glass, poised above me and ready to fall with one more shake of the kaleidoscope.

Chapter 9

Sometimes being homeschooled sucked.

Maybe that's too dramatic. I can't slam my education outright. Judging from the skills Heidi bragged about mastering during her high school years—how to affix a cheat sheet to the inside of a Coke bottle liner, how to argue any teacher from a D up to a C, how to use the surprisingly powerful words "I'm starting my period" to get out of an entire organic chemistry unit—I was probably learning more than most high schoolers. A lot more. Besides, my career wouldn't work without homeschool, and it had brought me Heidi.

But every once in a while I'd find myself in a situation

and realize I'd missed out, that I was supposed to know something I didn't know. Or worse, be somebody I didn't know how to be.

Standing on the front porch, for instance, listening to the taxi rumble away with Jeremy in the back, my insides churning and shaky, wishing I was still with him—that's when I felt it. I'd been studying the wrong things. I'd been wasting my time memorizing irregular French verbs and calculating the velocity of random trains leaving random stations at random times, when I should have been learning teenage survival skills: how to talk to a boy and not come across as a total idiot, how to flirt, how to lie to my parents. Why hadn't I said something charming or smiled or done *anything* besides just stumbling out onto the sidewalk like a half-baked loser?

It was so embarrassing. No, it was more than embarrassing—it was disturbing. My exposure to members of the opposite sex under the age of twenty-five was nearly nonexistent. That wasn't normal. Over the years there'd been a handful of guys that I knew and ran into at music festivals and competitions, but nobody romantically interesting, and definitely nobody I'd have actually let close enough to kiss me. I'd rather die than admit it to Heidi, who loved sharing the details of her dysfunctional relationships, but factoring in the higher-than-average gay-factor of male musicians, I had less experience than a cloistered nun.

As for my parent-handling skills, I was equally screwed. Diana and Clark were waiting on the other side of the door, and I had no game plan, no experience getting in trouble, and no guts. That *had* to be homeschool's fault. At the very least, public school would have given me front row seats to other people's misdemeanors and cover-ups.

With a hand on the brass knob, I closed my eyes and enjoyed one last breath of night air.

This situation was unprecedented, but I was pretty sure Diana was going to kill me. I should've been scared. Why wasn't I? Probably because my body was maxed out on euphoria. No room for fear. I felt like I was sucking on a half-dozen fizzy candies, and the mini-volcano was bubbling over into my brain. The street, the stars, the sound of the cicadas—everything was buzzing.

Think, Carmen. Fact: I was more likely to survive if I groveled than if I tried to excuse my way out of it. Diana hated excuses. Besides, what excuse could I possibly give? She knew me too well. She knew I wouldn't lie and sneak out over something trivial, and she knew I wouldn't be testing out rebellion just for fun.

But a logical defense just wouldn't come. My brain couldn't hold onto a single thought except the ones about Jeremy and that perfect, ringing, golden feeling of being kissed.

I twisted the knob and pushed, letting light pour out

onto the porch. The entryway was empty. They were probably in the living room, but I couldn't hear talking or TV or even music playing. That was a bad sign. There was always music playing. I forced myself forward, smelling coffee and Diana's vanilla sandalwood perfume. My heels clicked as they crossed the floor into the living room.

Clark sat on one end the sofa, arms folded over his chest, covering the peeling leprechaun logo on his favorite sweatshirt. Notre Dame. Go Irish. His face was gray and creased like weathered stone.

Something jagged punctured the bubble of elation inside me. Guilt. I'd been too scared of Diana to even think about Clark. He looked terrible, physically ill even, and it was my fault.

Clark shook his head slowly and glanced over to the antique chaise lounge where Diana was reclining. The brown velvet-backed chair was one of her favorites. Half-lying, half-sitting, she looked like she was posing for a painting, something to be entitled *Fainting Spell*, or *Ailing Mademoiselle*. Something dramatic.

Nobody spoke. We listened to the muted shriek of the same cicadas Jeremy and I had been listening to in the park, pulsing and insistent. Clark stared at Diana. Diana stared at me. I stared at the wall.

I looked down and saw the ticket stub in my hand, the perforated edge rubbed nearly smooth by my thumb. Why was I still holding it? Not exactly smart if I was going to lie about where I'd been. I held it up. A white flag.

"Enjoy yourself?" Diana said, her thin, scratchy voice no louder than usual. She ignored the ticket and held my gaze, her dark eyes simmering. I couldn't look away.

"Clark, honey," she continued, "you can go to bed. I need to talk to Carmen alone."

Not surprising. This was the unspoken arrangement of stepparenthood, at least in our family. Clark was a part of all things happy, but serious discussions were between Diana and me. Alone.

He sighed as he pushed himself out of the couch, relief softening his features. It was better this way. The tension was already eating him alive and we hadn't even started yet. It seemed fair at least to spare him, but I didn't want him to leave. He hugged me as he walked by, a too-tight squeeze, and whispered, "Don't *ever* scare us like that again."

I nodded, clinging to the faded sweatshirt. Unexpected tears filled my eyes and I squeezed them shut. I couldn't lose before I'd even started.

He detached himself and left. Diana and I listened to the creak of each step as he retreated upstairs. We were alone.

"He wanted to call the police," she said, "but I talked him out of it." Lines creased the lap of her jade-green dress, and the gold scarf sagged over her shoulders like a deflated sigh. She was still beautiful. Even with her lipstick faded to a muddy pink and the mascara smudged beneath her eyes.

She pushed herself up into a sitting position and turned to face me. Then she crossed her legs and the top one began bouncing rhythmically. My eyes broke away from her face and locked onto the gold stiletto that dangled from her toe.

"Well this is impressive," she said sarcastically. She was never sarcastic. "Lying, sneaking out, showing up at 3 a.m. like you don't have a care in the world. . . . You've outdone yourself, Carmen." She shook her head. "Honestly, I'm surprised. It's a little juvenile, don't you think?"

Jeremy thought so too.

"I'm sorry," I said, surprised to finally hear my own voice. "I didn't mean to worry you."

She rolled her eyes, another rarity. She never let me get away with that kind of thing. "You didn't worry me. You worried Clark." As she spoke, she took out the gold and ruby clusters hanging from her ear lobes and placed them on the end table beside her mug. "I knew exactly where you were. CSO concerts aren't exactly raves, so no, I wasn't worried. At least not about your physical safety." She waited for me to look her in the eye, but the shoe was just so much . . . safer. I looked back up at her face, which was now wrinkled with disappointment. "Carmen, what were you thinking?"

I was suddenly tired, too tired to think. I just wanted it over. "I don't know. I'm sorry."

"I can't understand you. The sneaking out was stupid, but what's worse is the complete disregard for your career. How do you think you're going to be feeling when you're walking onstage tomorrow night?"

She didn't want an answer. I lowered my eyes back to the glittering shoe, its arc wider and faster now.

"This is your last performance before the Guarneri. It should be a trial run for you, and based on what Yuri told me yesterday after your lesson, you should be focusing all your energy on figuring out why that concerto is slipping. By the way, why didn't *you* tell me that? I'm your *manager*."

The skin on my neck burned and I felt the flush bloom over my cheeks. Had Yuri called her to report how bad things were? Or had she called him?

"Because I can still fix it," I said. "I just have to . . ." What? She wanted a practical solution, but that was the problem. I was being strangled by all the practical solutions to the Tchaikovsky's descent into the graveyard of overplayed concertos.

"With your concerto withering before our eyes," she continued, "I can't imagine why you would choose right now to become obsessed with the *competition*. Why does it matter what Jeremy King sounds like? What did hearing how incredible he is do for your confidence?"

Shattered it, I thought, surprised that I'd forgotten. That part of the evening had slipped from my memory after everything that followed. After he kissed me. Suddenly, everything I'd felt during Jeremy's performance rushed back—the beauty, the sadness . . .

The realization that I would not win.

Diana turned her face away from me and put her hand to her throat, letting her fingertips rest on her scar, a shiny worm of a line sliding over her voice box. She stared out into the street, deliberating over something. "I heard him play last March when I was in New York."

The revelation took a moment to process. She'd lied. She'd come back from that trip and said she hadn't had time to go to the concert, that there had been some conflict with her schedule. "What? Why didn't you tell me?"

"Because I didn't want the legendary Jeremy King to undermine your confidence. You've always been the best. I needed you to keep believing that so you could win this thing. Now . . ." Her voice trailed off and she pulled her eyes from the window back to my face. "Well, it's too late for that now, isn't it?"

Her foot stopped swinging. The shoe slipped off her toe and clunked onto its side.

That was it. She thought I was fragile. She thought that just knowing how good he was would be too much, that I'd shut down and give up.

"The concert ended four hours ago. Where have you been?"

I glanced at her view out the window. She must have seen him in the back of the cab. Maybe she'd seen him kiss me. A spark of anger flickered inside me. Why was she asking if she'd seen the whole thing? And what made her think I would just give it up to her? That moment wasn't hers to poach.

But it didn't matter. I was done lying. "With Jeremy."

"Doing what?"

"Eating pizza in Millennium Park. Talking."

She raised an eyebrow. She *had* seen.

"How long ago did you meet him and why didn't you tell me about it?"

"I just met him after the concert tonight."

She narrowed her eyes.

"I'm telling the truth," I said evenly. No way was she getting the satisfaction of seeing how mad I was. "I went backstage and met him and he invited me to go get some dinner. We just started talking and lost track of time."

"Lost track of time? Four hours? *You* may have lost track of time. He didn't."

"I don't even know what you mean."

"Oh, Carmen," she groaned and pounded her palm to her forehead. "It's my own fault you're so naïve."

"Naïve?" Exasperation had crept into my voice, but I couldn't help it. She was being so vague and dramatic.

She sighed. "There are things about this business I've shielded you from, but I should have taught you to be more careful. Listen to me. People will do *anything* to win. You think that boy likes you, but he is not just some boy. He is here to win the Guarneri. He is not here to fall in love, though I'm sure he did a pretty convincing job of making you think that."

I said nothing. I froze my face. She was wrong. Of course she was wrong.

But even as one half of my brain repeated it, the other half cartwheeled backward through the evening, seeing a reverse reel of every event, every word and gesture. I flipped through it all, searching for evidence of just how ridiculously wrong, wrong, *wrong* she was. But there wasn't any.

"This competition will be close," she continued, "but it's between the two of you. Be smart, Carmen. He will do anything to derail you, including breaking your heart when you are at your most vulnerable."

No. The spark of anger inside me blossomed into flame. I wasn't that stupid. Jeremy wasn't like that.

"I can see you're mad," she said. "You should be. You don't deserve to be used. You're young and sweet and pretty, but your innocence is the problem. And now that you understand what's going on, you don't have to let him manipulate you like that."

I put my hand on the credenza to steady myself. It was glossy and cool beneath my skin. I felt like I might be sick.

"Listen to me, Carmen," she said, bringing me back into the moment. She was standing in front of me now and I could see her eyes were red. She brought both hands to my face and cupped my jaw. Her skin was soft and the smell of her perfume was stronger now. "Forget about Jeremy. Don't call him. Don't see him. Focus on the Tchaikovsky. We are *so* close to winning, Carmen. You just . . ." She dropped her hands. She wanted to finish the thought, but didn't. Couldn't.

I just . . .

I nodded weakly. "I know. I understand."

She turned away. "Good night."

Silently, I went upstairs.

Sleep was impossible. I should have been obsessing over my first kiss—the softness of his lips, his hand touching the back of my neck, the water-blue shade of his eyes—but Diana had killed that.

Instead, I analyzed every look and every word that led up to it. As evidence. He was a liar. If I told myself that, it was easy to see how everything that had happened could be woven into that story. That meant Jeremy was in his hotel bed right now, smiling, confident, relieved I was as gullible as he'd hoped, and plotting his next move. I hated him, more than I'd ever hated anyone or anything.

But what if Diana *was* wrong? Didn't I deserve to have this one normal thing?

I slipped out of my bed and crossed the hall to my studio. My case was open, my chin rest still attached from my last practice session. I picked up my violin and walked over to the window. A light rain had begun, bathing the window in a film of water, and the sky had turned from black to the darkest navy. Morning was coming. How had Jeremy described performing? Flying. Easy for him to say. Maybe he flew; I slogged. Tomorrow, or tonight now, I'd be slogging through lukewarm water on that same stage.

Unless . . .

The idea made the back of my neck tingle and my stomach drop. What would happen if I didn't take Inderal?

But you need it! my mind screamed. I did need it. Tokyo. Inderal saved me from that. But I also needed to change something and I was running out of time. Maybe what I needed was to jump, to freefall.

I put my violin up and played the opening phrase of the sweetest melody I could think of. It was Ralph Vaughan Williams' *The Lark Ascending.* Smooth and clean, the melody glided upward, lifting me with it. I closed my eyes and tried to remember the words to the poem that inspired the music. I couldn't. Yuri had made me memorize them, but that was years ago. I did remember the story, though. It was about a bird who flew up and up and up toward heaven until she was too high to be seen.

Chapter 10

have no scars. Not a one. Heidi says the ugly red mark on my neck and the calluses on my fingertips don't count because they'd go away after a few months if I were to stop playing. She's right. It seems like a deficiency though, like evidence of living life in a bubble.

Clark has several, the biggest being an eight-inch purple rope down the center of his knee from ACL surgery. The ski injury has a story behind it that involved a poorly placed mogul, a tree, and a spooked deer. I've heard it several dozen times, but never the same way twice.

My favorite of Clark's scars is the iridescent pink patch that wraps around the stub of his right pinky. He lost two digits at age fourteen to his uncle's table saw, but that wasn't what he told me when I was little. Back then he said he'd accidentally bitten it off in a hot dog eating contest. That really freaked me out. To this day, I'm a slow eater with finger foods.

Diana has just the one, the mother-of-pearl dash over her voicebox. I think it's kind of pretty, like a brushstroke. But she hates it. To her it's a sinister, worm-like reminder of a scalpel digging around in her throat for polyps. As if her scratchy voice isn't reminder enough.

Heidi has matching scars—glossy, pink patches over each elbow—from being chased by a dog on roller skates. She was the one on roller skates. Not the dog.

"I don't know why you are so obsessed with them," she said, as I examined the permanently damaged skin on her elbows, not for the first time.

It's simple though. I like the scars because I like the stories. Bravery, stupidity, pain—none of them come free.

"Is it weird that I don't have *any* scars?" I asked Diana once over a bowl of Raisin Bran.

"No, it's not weird. You don't have scars because you're graceful and spatially aware." She took a sip of coffee and added, "Not to mention young and lucky."

"But not a single one?"

Clark looked up from his newspaper. "It's because you're a slow eater," he said, lifting his four-and-a-half-fingered right hand and wiggling the stump. "Get over here and pinky swear to never enter a hot dog eating contest."

I laughed. Diana rolled her eyes. Clark shrugged and grinned, mission accomplished.

Operation Inderal detox was worse than I thought it would be.

I threw up twice. The first time was in the bathroom of my dressing room. Luckily, my hair was already up and hairsprayed into place so it didn't get splattered. Also luckily, Diana wasn't there to see it. If she had been, she might have guessed why I was puking and made me take a pill. I'd intentionally left my pillbox at home in case I chickened out, but I knew she kept an emergency stash in her purse.

I hadn't seen her all day. She'd left me to marinate in my shame, or whatever it was I was supposed to be feeling, while she ran errands. That was fine. I didn't want to talk to her either.

Clark dropped me off at Symphony Center two hours early, and drove off with his signature double-honk for good luck. He'd be in the audience later. Probably checking the score of the White Sox game on his phone every five minutes, but he'd be there.

And so would the Glenns. Apparently my grandparents had called last night and announced that they were in Chicago and would be attending the concert.

I made my way to the dressing room, the same one Jeremy had used, and tried to ignore the trembling in my hand as I reached for the knob. My fingers slid off twice before I managed to grip and twist. This was usually the peaceful part, arriving before the other musicians, feeling the quiet of the auditorium before a million melodic fragments clouded the air. My heart was already pumping too fast, aching behind my rib cage.

I just had to remind myself of what Dr. Wright had said: Inderal was not *physically* addictive. But if that was true, then this feeling that my body was about to explode or collapse or both was all in my head. If it was true, this pain in my gut was just neurosis.

Dr. Wright was full of crap.

Diana was supposed to meet me backstage with my dress an hour before call time.

My resolve was weakening. By the time she arrived, I was afraid I'd be begging her for Inderal.

Picking up my dress from Mei-Ling's, Diana's seamstress in Chinatown, was somewhere on her to-do list between buying pantyhose and going to Northwestern to drop off my music for the judges. (Ten days to go—original scores for all the Guarneri semifinalists were due.)

I'd performed in the dress only once before, but that

was over a year ago. It had needed letting out in the bust, a discovery we'd made thanks to Diana's fixation with seeing me in performing dresses three weeks early, just in case lipstick stains had to be removed or hems re-stitched. Both she and Heidi had insisted it was too tight, which Heidi reinforced by referring to me as Dolly Parton for several days. So we'd all gone to Mei-Ling's for a fitting. Heidi had come along so we could work on physics in the car, but spent most of the time writing haikus on the edges of my notebook about hating General Electric (home of her most recently botched job interview), while Diana talked on the phone with her travel agent about the price of flights to Sydney in August. That was the last time I'd seen the dress. I'd brought a spare just in case, but I liked the other one better. It was white, and white seemed like the right color for a fresh start.

My warm-up inched by. I practiced, I did my hair, I practiced, I started to feel shaky, I started to feel nauseous, I did my makeup, I tried to think about happy things like the beach and chocolate ice cream, I ended up wondering if Jeremy would be in the audience, I threw up, I practiced, I paced, I did this windmill thing with my arms to try to force the blood to my fingertips, and then I practiced a little more. Not having Diana there at least gave me something concrete to stress about. Getting nervous about getting nervous was just too abstract to get a grip on, but I could freak out about not having my dress arrive and that felt much better.

What am I doing? The thought seized my brain every few minutes, and I'd try to smother the panic with some relaxation exercises Dr. Wright had suggested at my follow-up appointment: deep breaths, calm thoughts, deep breaths, calm thoughts, deep breaths, calm thoughts. Dr. Wright really was full of crap.

At fifteen minutes to go, I started pacing faster, this time in a wide loop around the dressing room: between the coffee table and the sofa, over the ottoman, around the piano, down the mirrored wall, repeat. My legs shook under me, but the repetition was oddly numbing. An image of the polar bears in the Lincoln Park Zoo came to my mind, lumbering pitifully around their cages in the same circuit over and over. Maybe they had anxiety issues too.

Where was she? Diana was never late, so being late to a *performance* was completely unthinkable. My stomach still hurt from the puking. Would she be able to tell? I looked in the mirror. Scary. My skin was an eerie greenish-white, my stage makeup even more garish than usual. Glossy red lipstick, green eye shadow over blood-shot eyes—I looked like a circus clown with the stomach flu. I'd taken off my shirt before hair and makeup, and was wearing just jeans and a bra, adding another layer of weird to the image in the mirror. How could Jeremy kiss that face?

I opened the closet and took out the dress bag holding my backup, a navy blue organza dress with a sweetheart neckline. I was deciding whether I should put it on or go back to the bathroom to throw up again, when the door swung open.

"You wouldn't believe traffic," Diana gasped, twirling around to hang the dress bag on the hook behind the door and tossing a Sak's Fifth Avenue bag on the sofa in one breathless movement. "I almost forgot the pantyhose," she added and pulled a package of sheer control-tops out of her purse.

I grabbed the garment bag and unzipped it, in too much of a hurry to hide my shaking hands. It was like I remembered, simple but dramatic, the color of milk, strapless, with a wide blood-red sash tied around the waist. It was the kind of dress that drew eyes in and held them. I took off my jeans, put on the pantyhose, and pulled on the dress. It fit perfectly.

I looked in the mirror again. The image was less scary. The dress was stunning. My lips and the sash looked like they'd been dipped in the same dye, and the sickly shade of my skin was definitely less noticeable.

Over my shoulder, Diana's reflection frowned at me. I turned away.

My fingers. I had to stop the shaking. I picked up my violin to do one last round of shifting drills. They were ugly and whiny (according to Clark, the drills sound exactly like the noise a cat makes when you swing it around by the tail), but they helped get the blood pumping to my fingers.

Diana changed into her own outfit, a long tight mauve dress, while pretending not to watch me. I kept up the cat wrangling and pretended not to notice her pretending not to watch me.

A knock at the door startled us both. "Five minutes," a muffled male voice called from the hallway.

My stomach lurched, and my knees buckled. I would have fallen but my elbow caught the edge of the piano and I leaned into the instrument to steady myself.

"Carmen!" Diana cried. Was her voice always so shrill? "Are you okay?"

"I'm fine."

"Did you forget to eat?"

"Um . . ." That was a pretty good excuse, actually. "Yeah."

She commenced rifling through her purse, and nattering about the physical effects of low blood sugar and the importance of planning ahead. By the time her rant had come full circle, she'd unearthed a Luna bar, three Certs, and a package of black licorice. She made me eat it all.

"It's time," she said.

I choked down the last piece of licorice and washed my hands in the sink, letting the scalding water pour over my skin. Maybe that would heat them up. But by the time I'd twisted the faucet off and dried my hands, my fingers were cold again.

Why was I doing this? Why hadn't I just taken the Inderal like I was supposed to? But it didn't matter now. It was too late.

Diana followed me down the corridor that led to the stage right curtain. A handful of people stood waiting—the conductor, Maestro Chang, giving directions to the stage manager; a new technician I didn't recognize; a stage hand with two metal music stands tucked under each arm. I stood a little apart from the cluster, took a shaky breath, and closed my eyes.

I tried to focus, but the music in my head had never been quite so dizzying. Rolling waves of melodic passages overlapped, Tchaikovsky's beautiful themes all mashing together unnaturally. I felt like I was standing on a rocking boat and staring into a warped mirror at the same time. It was a discordant nightmare.

Suddenly, my mouth felt wet and I knew. I shoved my violin into Diana's hands and gave my surroundings a panicky search for something to throw up into. There was nothing. I was about to lose it when I saw the trash can and rushed over, reaching it just in time. *Why couldn't I be doing this alone?* I thought as I retched into the can. Even in the middle of those slow-motion spasms, I was aware of at least five pairs of eyes on me, of Diana's hand resting on my back, of the dissonant jumble of notes still swirling in my head, of the fact that I still had to perform. One Luna bar, three Certs, a package of black licorice. Of course, she *had* to make me eat them all. I was done. My jaw ached.

"Feel better?" Diana asked. Her voice was small and hard like a pebble.

"No." I didn't. I felt weak.

"I wonder why."

She knew.

I forced myself to look at her, still gripping the trash can, bracing for her fury. But she didn't look mad. Her mouth was slightly open, her eyes watery, her brows arched like she was in pain. She looked wounded, like I'd kicked her in the stomach.

"Why?" Her voice quivered as she spoke. "Why would you do this *now?*"

She was about to cry. I stared at her, but I didn't feel anything. At first. Then the anger came, falling on me like a flood of fire. *She thinks I'm punishing her.*

"It's not about you," I hissed, and pulled my violin out of her hands. The venom made my voice sound like someone else's. I'd never talked to her like that before. "Why does it always have to be about you?"

Diana put her hand to her cheek and wiped a tear. It was a *poor me* move, but it had the opposite effect. I couldn't feel sorry for her. And did she actually think a guilt trip would fix things now?

"Of course it's not about *me*," she said. "I know exactly who this is about. I know who inspired this, this"—she shook her head as she fumbled for the words—"career-ending *stupidity*. Let me guess, he told you that taking Inderal was slowing you down. Or did he tell you it wasn't fair? Either way, you're about to find out just how much Jeremy King actually cares about you."

The anger exploded in my chest, strong and hot, pushing my heart out and up against my rib cage. The passive aggressive act was one thing, but blaming Jeremy . . .

Without thinking, I lifted my foot and drove my heel into the wood stage, aware as pain shot up my shin that I was acting like a five-year-old. Miraculously, the tall skinny heel didn't snap. I turned to see my small crowd of backstage onlookers, staring, mouths open. Lucky them. They had the best, or at least the most fascinating, seats in the house: first a puke-fest and now a catfight. I glared right at them, still too mad to be ashamed.

I took two steps away from Diana, toward the group at the edge of the stage. "It's time," I announced, and for the first time since I'd arrived at the Symphony Center my voice didn't shake.

I squeezed my fingers into balls and pumped them a few times. They weren't cold anymore. My whole body felt hot and strong, like I could punch a hole through a wall. The feeling beat fear, but was still dangerous. I'd never played this angry before. I'd never *been* this angry before.

Without looking at Diana, I walked to the curtain's edge and stared out into the audience. Her reasoning stung. She assumed Jeremy had convinced me not to take Inderal, that *somebody* had to be telling me what to do. It was impossible for her to believe that I'd made the decision for myself.

The stage manager murmured something into his microphone and the house lights dimmed. The musicians put their instruments in their laps, leaving just the sound of my own heart pumping in my ears. The concertmaster stood and signaled for the oboist's A. The orchestra tuned.

Even worse than the insinuation that Jeremy had talked me into not taking Inderal, even worse than the suggestion that I had told him I used it, *she thought I had no chance without it.* My grip tightened around the neck of my violin. For the first time in a long time I had a definitive goal onstage. I was going to prove her wrong.

I turned to the conductor who was waiting to walk

onstage too. He grimaced. The professional thing to do would have been to give him a reassuring smile. After all, he had just seen me puke into a trash can and yell at my mother, but I didn't feel like being professional. I felt like screaming obscenities and snapping my bow in half over my knee.

The stage manager cleared his throat and gestured to the stage. I nodded and without thinking charged forward, still squeezing the neck of my violin.

"She's walking," was the last thing I heard him say into his microphone, and then an explosion of applause engulfed me. Was it always this loud? This bright? The bows of the musicians fluttered spasmodically, their own version of clapping. Was the movement always so frantic?

My legs propelled me to center stage. When I reached my spot I closed my eyes to tune, then glanced sideways across the stage to the curtain's edge where she stood, arms folded, head bowed. She was in the shadow, but her outline was clear. She thought she owned me. She thought the success or the failure of this performance had something to do with her.

I glanced into the audience. Was he out there? I didn't know whether to hope so or not.

The conductor cleared his throat, and I glared back at him. *Where's the fire, buddy?* I tried saying with just my eyes. *Can I not take just a second to think?* I'd never been rude to a conductor before, but it didn't feel terrible. It was kind of empowering.

His eyes rolled up, up to the ornate ceiling, saying *Why me?*, then he drove his baton downward.

The music began, and miraculously, my ear anchored itself to the sound. I'd traded fear and all its slipperiness for anger. Not a single note was going to get away from me.

My entrance came and I nailed it. The strings felt razor-sharp beneath my fingers, but the pain was reassuring, fueling even. Being mad and strong meant being in control.

Anger propelled me through the first movement, but dissipated into self-pity by the time I reached the slow second movement. The sadness behind the melody suddenly made sense. My own pitiful life—hating Jeremy, then not hating Jeremy, kissing him, then realizing that the Guarneri made an *us* impossible, and of course Diana's accusations—gave me a tragedy to feel. Maybe for the first time.

The final movement was a wild one. I'd always pictured galloping horses, the way my bow bounced reminding me of hooves striking the ground and kicking off again and again. Tonight the horses were on a death-sprint. From beyond my scroll, the conductor shot me an alarmed look. We hadn't rehearsed it this fast—I'd never even heard anyone play it this fast—but his baton followed my pace. Finally, the exhilaration of the music took over and I realized I wasn't angry or sad anymore. The blur of notes flew from my own hands, faster than I could even think them. This was what Jeremy had been talking about, the almost-done.

I tossed the final chords of the concerto upward into the hall with a gasp of relief. It was over. The cries of "Bravo!" began before I'd even opened my eyes and my entire body rang with the adrenaline. I was flying.

I emailed Jeremy as soon as I was alone in my bedroom, before I even took off my dress.

Are you still looking for a tour guide?

-C

The minute I pressed send I wanted to take it back. Why didn't email have a sixty second take-it-back option? This was the downside of the adrenaline high. I was too wired to sleep and too giddy to think things through.

The wait for a reply was agonizing. Maybe I should have texted instead. He was probably already asleep. Still, I checked my inbox every two minutes. In between hitting the refresh button I hung up my dress, put my pajamas on, listened to Clark make himself a snack in the kitchen and Diana brush her teeth, reorganized the shoes in my closet,

replayed the highlights of the performance in my mind . . .
and then there it was.

> Of course. I'm kind of surprised you're
> offering—I thought the leash was too tight.

> Jeremy

I typed my reply quickly.

> I'm rethinking the leash. It might only be as
> tight as I let it. Were you in the audience
> tonight?

I stared at the screen for a full minute before I pressed
send. Asking seemed so desperate. If he had been there he
probably would have come backstage, but maybe he *had*
been there and just hadn't stayed. Maybe he'd had to leave
right away. I pressed send.

It felt like an eternity before he responded.

> Wasn't there. Sorry. I'll explain in person.
> How'd it go? When do I get to see you?

He hadn't come. That was probably good, preferable
even, as far as the Guarneri was concerned.

Except that tonight's performance had been so personal. If he'd been there, maybe he would understand me completely, understand things I could never just explain with words.

It didn't matter.

It went well. Want to see a baseball game?
The White Sox play on Wednesday and my
stepdad has season tickets.

A brutal silence followed. I stared at the blinking cursor, wondering how this had gotten turned around, how I'd ended up feeling like the one doing the chasing. *He* was the one who'd wanted me to take him around, *he* was the one who had kissed me . . .

I'd love to. He's not using them?

Interesting question. It was opening week and Clark did love his Sox. He'd already sacrificed tonight's game to go to my concert, but Wednesday night was a CSO fund-raising banquet and Diana was on the organizing committee. They had debated it all the way home from the concert, but I'd only been half listening. I'd been too busy savoring my victories: I hadn't taken Inderal; I hadn't bombed; the Tchaikovsky was alive again; and Diana had been so, so wrong. I was only vaguely aware of Clark's losing battle in the background. He argued that he spent more time at the symphony than any tone deaf man in the world, so he didn't see why he had to give up another Sox game to listen to people *talk* about the symphony. She got passive aggressive, then he called her on it, and so on, until she ended it with, "I'm co-chairing the damn thing. We're going to the benefit." And then things had gone quiet.

I typed my response, feeling bad for Clark.

No. He has leash issues.
So, I guess I'll see you on Wednesday.

I pulled my eyes away from the computer screen. Sometime during the last hour my head had started to ache and now it was approaching pounding. I had forgotten about this feeling. The adrenaline that had carried me all night was finally waning, which meant I would crash. I smiled. The postperformance low—more evidence that I'd done it. Without Inderal.

A surge of energy coursed through me. Never again. I wasn't *ever* taking that drug again. I grabbed the pillbox from my bedside table and ran to my bathroom. I was done being a coward. I twisted off the lid, held the open pillbox out over the toilet, and tipped it. The pills hit the water and sank like orange confetti. One flush. They swirled and swirled and swirled and disappeared.

I climbed into bed, curled my body around my pillow, and started replaying the best parts of the night. Then the best parts of last night with Jeremy. This time, I remembered it as it had happened, without any of the doubts and second-guessing and sabotage Diana had thrown in. That was over.

The sound of my phone from across the room pulled me from my thoughts. Heidi was the only person who would call me this late. She was either calling to see how the performance went or to tell me about some lame Lifetime Network weekend movie she had just watched. She had a weakness for those. I crossed the room and fished the phone from my purse.

It wasn't Heidi's number. It was Jeremy's.

I took a shaky breath and pressed talk. "Hi."

"Did I wake you?"

"No."

"Are you lying?"

"No, I performed tonight. I'm still jittery."

"Good. I mean that you weren't sleeping, not that you're jittery."

"Yeah."

Silence. Was I supposed to say something now? My mind was blank. Phone to my ear, I crawled back into bed and stared at the ceiling.

"So, I don't really know why I'm calling."

"Hmmm," I said, then laughed.

Then he laughed too. "Awkward, huh?"

"Email's easier," I admitted.

"But different," he said. "It's nice to hear your voice."

I wanted to say it was nice to hear his. I almost let myself.

"I guess that's why I called," he said, "to hear your voice."

"Actually, I was just sitting here thinking about the other night." Had I just said that? *Less honesty, Carmen.* I could hear him smiling in the silence, if that was even possible. He was thinking about the kiss too.

"So we're on for Wednesday?" I asked.

"The baseball game? Yeah. That sounds great. But . . ."

"But what?" I braced myself for an excuse. Something along the lines of: *but I think spending time with you is pure poison to my competition head game.*

"But Wednesday seems like a long ways away."

Four days. It *did* seem like a long ways away, like forever. And he thought so too.

"Can I see you tomorrow?" he asked.

"Tomorrow?" What did Diana have set up for tomorrow? The thought wiggled its way in before I remembered I didn't give a crap. I had to do better than that. Ten minutes ago I'd been basking in my glorious freedom, and now I was looking to reattach the severed apron strings? "Yeah, tomorrow is good. What do you want to do?"

"I don't know. Is it warm enough for the beach?"

"Are you kidding? It snowed yesterday."

"Yeah, but it warmed right up afterward."

"It's too cold to swim, but not too cold to go to the beach and make fun of the Canadian tourists for swimming."

"Tempting," he said, "but I've got a better idea."

"Okay, let's hear it."

"I think I'm keeping it a secret."

"How am I supposed to know what to wear?"

"That's easy. Wear something sexy."

"What? Where are we going that I would have to be wearing something sexy?"

"Has nothing to do with where we're going. I just think you should wear something sexy."

I couldn't quite come up with a response.

"You're blushing, aren't you."

"No. Why would I be blushing?" I was blushing.

"Because I think you talk tough but that you're shy, and I just embarrassed you."

"I . . . I . . ."

"It's okay. You're blushing. Don't worry about it."

"Shut up."

"As soon as you agree to meet me tomorrow night at the State and Lake train station."

"What time?"

"Nine."

That would be tricky. Diana and Clark would be home. *Good thing I no longer fear confrontation?* "Nine it is."

"Good. Still blushing?"

"I never was."

"Whatever."

"Good night, Jeremy."

"Good night, Carmen."

"Carmen."

I opened my eyes. It was dark, but enough moonlight glowed from the window to illuminate Diana's profile. She was sitting on my bed, staring at the row of framed pressed flowers on the wall. We'd picked the poppies together in Nonna's garden in Milan, and pressed them between pages of a fat volume of poetry when we got back to the States. That had been three summers ago, at the end of my first European tour.

It took a moment to clear the sleepy haze mixed with Italy and wildflowers and Nonna's homemade gnocchi from my head, but then I remembered last night and smiled in the dark.

"Carmen," she whispered again.

"What?"

She rested a hand on my calf and turned to face me. Her eyes were glossy, her cheeks puffy and raw. She'd been crying. I'd made her cry.

"I'm sorry," she said.

I waited, but she didn't say more. Maybe that was good. I could assume she was sorry for everything: for the pressure, for pushing Inderal on me, for not believing I could play without it, and for the things she had said about Jeremy. That's what I wanted.

"It's okay."

The words punctured something in her and she deflated before me, dropping her head to into her hands like it was too heavy to keep holding up. Her shoulders began to bounce up and down rhythmically. I wanted to look away, but I couldn't. I'd never seen her cry before, or at least not like this. It was terrible. The only sounds she made were little gasps between shoulder jerks, but the slumped posture, the disheveled hair, the entire scene was painful to watch. She was supposed to be unbreakable.

"It's okay," I repeated lamely. What was I supposed to do? I sat up and put my arm around her, hoping she'd straighten her back and be Diana again.

"No," she answered, her gravelly voice low and bitter. She shook her head and pulled her fingers up to the scar on her throat. "It's not."

Our eyes locked, but hers were dark and unreadable. Then the thought occurred as I stared into them: Maybe she was sorry about something else entirely. Something that had nothing to do with me.

Flowers arrived around ten o'clock the next morning. Stalks and stalks of pink gladiolas, their huge heads piled one over the other, toppling out over the floral cellophane. The card was typed.

Carmen,
Lovely, lovely, lovely. You played like an angel. Make us
proud next week.
Thomas and Dorothy Glenn

Chapter 11

Slipping out on a Sunday night should have been tricky. The fact that it wasn't made me consider the possibility that fate was on my side, which then made me wonder if my attempts at being a pseudo-Catholic were pointless. God had already shown he wasn't exactly behind me, but *fate*, and being a *fatalist*. . . . That sounded much more promising. Fate brings lovers together. Fate is very operatic. Then again, sometimes those fated lovers in operas turn out to be siblings or destined to die in a tomb together or kill each other accidentally.

Regardless, Clark and Diana left in a cab at seven

thirty and they wouldn't be back until at least one in the morning, probably later. If the last time they went out with Clark's pack of "Domers" was any indication, they'd be just tipsy enough to go straight to bed.

Just in case, I did stuff my bed with pillows, but more for the experience, to be able to say I'd done it, than because it was actually necessary.

I arrived at the train station five minutes late. I'd had to try on everything in my closet three times before I realized there was no right outfit. Nothing in Diana's closet worked either. There was too sexy or not sexy enough. I ended up in skinny jeans and a fitted angora sweater, but thinking I probably should've stayed with the pencil skirt and belted denim jacket. Maybe neither was particularly sexy. Maybe I had no clue.

Jeremy was waiting at the turnstile, smiling, probably because he knew he looked good in his green sweater and indigo jeans, and hadn't had to try on everything he owned to prove it. "Hey," he said.

I felt like I had a tennis ball stuck in my throat—why didn't he look nervous? "Hey."

"Ready to go?" He held out a train ticket for me. Was he really not going to comment on my outfit? His smile was easy, casual, clueless. Nope. He was not.

"Depends," I said. "Where are we going?"

"I can't tell you."

"Well, then maybe I can't go with you."

He squinted and folded his arms over his chest, surveying the slow trickle of Sunday night travelers. "How about I give you a hint instead."

"Sure. I'm sure a hint's all I need anyway."

"You think you're pretty smart then?" he said, his voice somewhere between playful and cocky.

"I only have to be smarter than *you* think I am, right?" I followed him through the turnstile and down the stairs to the platform.

"Well, now I'm in a position where I have to make it impossibly hard if I don't want to insult you. That wasn't smart at all."

"Oh, wow, just give me the hint already."

"Okay, okay," he said. "We're going to a piano concert."

"That's not a hint at all. You just told me where we're going."

"I know. I cracked under all that hint-talk pressure."

I looked down at my pants and sweater. "And I'm too casual, thanks a lot."

We stepped onto the train and the doors slid shut. "No, you're dressed perfectly," he said, looking at me for the first time. I felt his hand on the side of my waist, guiding me to the nearest row of seats. Everything inside me melted. It was impossible to feel his touch without thinking about kissing him again, and impossible to engage in normal conversation when I was doing that. Where were we going again? A concert. A piano concert.

"Who's playing?"

"No, the rest is still a secret."

I frowned at the El map above me. "Where is this concert? Do you know where you're going?"

"Uptown, and I'll try not to be insulted by the suggestion that I can't navigate Chicago's public transport."

It was easier to talk to him when we were beside each other like this, close, touching, but without the awkwardness of staring into each other's eyes. Except it might be nice to look into his eyes.

"But we must be going in the wrong direction. I can't think of a single concert venue this way."

"Carmen," he said and turned to face me. I had no choice but to look up at him, to stare into his eyes just inches away from mine. They were a stormier version of blue than I'd remembered. "Can't you just trust me?"

The pause was too long. I was distracted by the newness of everything, his smell, the feeling of being looked at like that, the warmth of his leg beside mine. And maybe I didn't know how to answer the question. "I don't know."

"Try."

We got off at Lawrence, and Jeremy held my hand as we walked through the kind of neighborhood Diana and Clark would have locked the car doors when driving through. After a few blocks of sketchy buildings and sketchier people, I vaguely recognized the name on a neon green sign up ahead and realized we were at our destination. The Green Mill. It was a famous jazz club, but nothing like the concert venues I was used to.

"Jeremy, I'm not twenty-one," I said, before I realized how dumb that sounded. Neither was he.

"It's okay. I know the bouncer."

"How do you know the bouncer? I didn't think you knew anyone in Chicago."

"I don't really, but I came here the other night because I'd heard the music was incredible. He wouldn't let me in, but then I noticed he had a Manchester United scarf, so we got to talking about football—or soccer, whatever—and it turns out he used to live in London. Anyway, I convinced him I was here for the music and not for the liquor and he let me in."

We were standing outside the entrance now. "You've really never been here before?"

I shook my head. "I've *heard* of it, but never actually been here."

"Brilliant," he said. He looked like a little boy, all excited and proud of himself. "You're going to love it."

"I don't know a thing about jazz."

"That's okay." He pulled me toward the door and opened it. "You know music. Jazz will explain itself.

Mikey!" Jeremy grabbed the hand of the mammoth man standing guard at the door. He was about Jeremy's height and at least double the weight, wearing a leather jacket, a pinky ring, and an earpiece with a microphone. Basically, a textbook bouncer.

"You're back!" he exclaimed. "Dude, you just missed the Poetry Slam."

"Oh, that's okay," Jeremy said. "We're here for the music, right?"

I nodded, feeling more than a little out of my element. Poetry Slam sounded a little aggressive to me, almost violent.

Mikey examined me. "Dude, I don't know if I can let the chick in," he said, shaking his head.

"Carmen? No, she's cool. Look, neither of us are drinking."

"Yeah, but it doesn't work like that. At least you look twenty-one. She looks fourteen. Barely."

So the outfit was definitely *not* sexy enough. I considered giving Mikey a piece of my almost-eighteen-year-old mind, but his physical presence (the prison tattoos on his forearms, a neck the size of my waist) had a dampening effect on my irritation.

"I know she looks pretty milk-toast, but would you believe she's got the Manchester United crest tattooed on her?"

Mikey squinted at me. "Where?"

Jeremy laughed. "I can't tell you that. Use your imagination."

Mikey shook his head. "I'm pretty sure that's a felony. Fine. Go ahead. Just promise next time you're at a soccer game you'll think of me."

"Of course," Jeremy said and pushed me through the door before Mikey could change his mind.

"Milk-toast? What's that supposed to mean?" I said.

"Um, boring."

I didn't have time to be insulted. I was being sucked through a time warp into a 1920s speakeasy. My eyes adjusted to the dark and took in the clusters of people. Women in satiny dresses and fishnet stockings, men in gangster suits and matching hats—was this all real? And the music. My other senses quieted as I focused everything on its elements: a rumbly-voiced woman, fingers trickling over a keyboard, the teasing beat of a bass drum and cymbal. Hypnotic, but totally foreign. Soulful and strong, weightless and easy, all at the same time.

"This is the oldest jazz club in the country," Jeremy said into my ear, and I felt his breath on my neck, bringing me out of one dream and into another. I looked around. The Green Mill was busy, but not too loud. Conversations were hushed so people could hear the music.

"This is unreal," I said. "I feel like I'm on a movie set."

"I know. Amazing isn't it? I'm so glad you've never been here. I like surprising you."

Our waitress, a slight woman with fake eyelashes and a soft voice, led us across the dark lounge to one of the velvet booths at the edge of the room. Not everyone, I noticed as we walked the length of the bar, was glammed up in Prohibition-era garb, but enough to make the whole place feel strangely authentic.

I slid into the booth. Jeremy sat across from me.

"So you know jazz," I said, and gave him an intentionally suspicious squint.

He shrugged. "Not really."

"I don't believe you."

"Let's just say I'm a relatively new listener."

"Just a fan or do you play?"

"I'm a musician. I don't think I could be just a fan. Trust me, by the end of the night you'll be wanting to play jazz too."

"So grab an instrument and get up there," I teased, gesturing to the stage. "Let's hear what you got."

"What, and commit career suicide?" he joked. "What would my classical fans think?"

"Fair enough."

Jeremy looked up on stage where a new group of musicians was getting ready to perform. "This is the piano combo I heard the other night. This guy is amazing. A genius. He almost makes me wish I could really play the piano."

"There are plenty of jazz violinists."

"Maybe. But nobody wants to be that guy."

"What guy?" I asked, knowing exactly what he was talking about.

"The one accused of bastardizing classical music to cater to a wider audience."

"Oh, that guy."

We both knew the rules. The classical music industry is run by snobs, and musicians who try to spice up their images aren't taken seriously, even if it isn't just for their image. Even if it's because they want to test out jazz. We have agents and managers, recording contracts with major labels, teachers and mentors to make sure we don't do stupid things like moonlight at Chicago jazz clubs.

"I don't know," I said. "I think maybe you should try bucking a few trends. How about for your next CD you record half bluegrass fiddle music and the other half New Age-y stuff. You could be doing yoga in overalls for the cover art."

"Sure. And for your next CD I'm going to recommend you play only Metallica songs and for the photo you should be playing an electric violin and wearing a bikini."

"So tell me what you know about jazz," I said, changing the subject.

"Fine, no bikini."

A woman had joined the pianist on stage, a flute in her hand. She sat on a stool with her eyes closed, nodding her head and pulsing with her whole upper body to the beat. The percussionist seemed to be dancing with his drum set, but mostly just listening to the melody on the keyboard. I closed my eyes to listen. The melody meandered but pushed along gently too. I could sit here all night.

When I opened my eyes, Jeremy was looking at me.

"Hungry?" he asked.

"All of the sudden, yeah. Is the food good?"

"Really good."

On his recommendation, I ordered the fried ravioli; he had scallops in an avocado sauce and we shared an order of gorgonzola stuffed mushrooms.

"I found out about this place online," Jeremy said between bites. "I realized I was going to be here in Chicago for a few weeks before the competition, so I went looking for stuff to do so I didn't get bored—did I tell you Al Capone used to hang out here?"

"Seriously?"

"Yeah, it used to be owned by mobsters," he said and gestured to the black-and-white photos on the walls.

"Do you want a bite of my ravioli?" I asked.

"Sure. And go ahead and try the scallops."

I reached across him with my fork for a bite of his food. "Is it weird being in Chicago by yourself?"

"No. I've been on tour alone before. It's not so bad. I get to find cool places like this, which I probably wouldn't get to do if I had someone hovering."

"My mother tours with me," I said. "We have fun, but she's more of a museum/botanical gardens/spa treatment type of traveler. Nothing like this." I waved my fork around. "It isn't lonely, though?"

"Sometimes. Not now." His eyes were smiling.

The image of how he'd looked when he walked onstage Friday—arrogant and surly and rude—flashed in my mind. It was so different from what was in front of me. *This* had to be the real Jeremy.

Didn't it?

"Now you owe me," he said.

"How so?"

"Well, you know something about me that almost nobody else knows—the jazz, I mean. You owe me something I can't read in your bio or if I google you."

"You google me?"

"I said *if* I google you. And you're changing the subject again."

I put my fork down on my plate. One last ravioli

remained, but I was too full. What could I tell him? Everything un-violin in my life seemed so lame. "My stepdad and I run together," I blurted out.

He sat patiently, obviously waiting for me to go on.

"For some reason he doesn't get that violin is the defining element in my life and is always trying to get me to branch out. So, we run six or seven miles or sometimes even ten miles a couple of times a week. We were going to run a marathon together in June, but I couldn't train properly this spring. He's running it without me."

"A marathon. That's forty-two kilometers, right?" he asked.

"Twenty-six point two miles. The marathon he's running is in South Bend, Indiana, and the finish line is inside the Notre Dame football stadium. He went to school there and he's a sports fanatic so that stadium is his place of worship. It's pretty much like Mecca for him. Anyway, I'll run one someday."

"That's amazing."

I shrugged. "I don't know if I can actually do it yet. The most I've ever run is twelve."

"But, I don't get it. It's fun?"

I laughed. "Actually, yeah. Or it's fun to do it with Clark. It's kind of like violin, actually."

"How so?"

"It's hard. Sometimes it hurts. Some days I really have

to force myself to do it, but those are usually the days I feel the best afterward."

"So why doesn't your mom want you to do it?"

"She just wants me to be doing other things this summer. I know I can fit the runs in, but she doesn't think I can train and . . . You know . . ."

The Guarneri. The winner would be on tour by then. Jeremy nodded. We couldn't avoid it, even when we tried.

"Have you ever had time for a sport?" I asked, wishing that hard look hadn't crept into his eyes again.

"I used to play rugby, but the insurance blokes put a stop to that."

I resisted the urge to laugh at the word bloke and just nodded.

"Jerks, eh?" he continued. "They insure your hands and then think they have right to tell you not to let thugs in cleats jump on them."

"Mine are insured too, but my extracurriculars don't involve thugs in cleats so I generally don't have a problem."

A lull in the conversation made me realize how much time had passed. It felt like we'd just sat down, but our plates had almost emptied and a different group was onstage playing. I wanted to freeze time. Maybe then we could stay as these versions of ourselves, and Jeremy would never have to turn back into the guy I'd seen on stage. The guy who could take everything from me.

"Why don't you get nervous when you perform?" I asked.

"Why don't *you* get nervous?" The edge had crept back in.

There was no acceptable answer to that question. I couldn't tell him about Inderal, I wouldn't admit that I did get nervous, I didn't want to lie and tell him I didn't . . . "I asked you first."

"I *do* get nervous. Really, really nervous, as in throwing up. I spent a good year having terrible performances when I was thirteen. It just hit me all of the sudden, you know? I'd been performing my whole life, obviously, but suddenly I was aware of everything that was just automatic before. And not just the physical stuff. Aware of people's expectations. Of my expectations."

"But you don't seem nervous on stage. At all."

He gave a wry smile. "You mean my shtick?"

"I probably wouldn't have called it that, but, yeah."

"It gives me something to focus on. Having a role to play helps."

"Jeremy . . ." I let my voice trail off without even trying to say what had to be said.

"What?"

"I don't know."

"Sure you do. What?"

"You're making it impossible to hate you again."

"But I thought we'd already decided it was okay to not hate each other."

"I don't know. I thought we'd decided we might have to." I picked up my fork and pushed the remaining ravioli around, making patterns in the sauce.

He sighed. "So you don't get nervous then. What's your secret?"

"No secret."

"Lucky."

I shrugged. All the lines I'd been fed by Diana and Dr. Wright about Inderal turned magically into what they had always been. Dust. Stories. It was cheating. Maybe I'd always known, but it didn't matter now, because I wasn't taking it ever again. I'd survived last night without it, hadn't I? The Guarneri would be scary as hell without it, but that was the way it had to be. Jeremy's description of performing had shaken something loose, something I'd always known but forgotten. Nerves were normal. Real musicians learned how to deal with them.

I turned to the stage where the music had stopped. The singer was getting ready to saunter off, but first gave her two fingers a kiss and tossed it to the crowd.

The lightness I'd felt all night was gone. It had deserted me somewhere between jazz combos and performance talks. I needed more. I needed to put my head on Jeremy's chest and for him hold me and tell me that the next week wasn't going to end in disaster.

Our waitress came and cleared our plates and refilled our drinks. "Dessert?" she asked and left a dessert menu with our choices before we could say no.

"Want to split the tiramisu?" he asked.

"I don't know. What time is it?"

Jeremy checked his watch. "One-thirty."

"I need to get home."

Jeremy nodded but didn't look at me. He felt it too. Something had changed.

"They look so free," I said, gesturing toward the musicians onstage.

"I know."

"I'm sorry," he said. "I didn't realize it was so late. Will your parents be mad?"

I shook my head.

He paid for our meal and we pushed our way through the crowd to the door.

I hadn't realized how warming the smoke and jazz were until Jeremy opened the door to the street and the icy wind cut into me.

Before I could open my mouth to complain, Jeremy was taking off his sweater.

"You'll be cold . . ." I started to say, but it sounded unconvincing, so I let my words trail off. Wearing just a black T-shirt, he hailed a cab, while I pulled his sweater over my head.

"What's the matter?" he asked once we were settled in the cab, pulling me close. His body felt warm against mine and my shivering melted away. "Did I say something wrong?"

"No. I'm just sad. I think I want more than I can have."

He stared silently out the window, his eyes following the lights of buildings we passed.

This time when we pulled up in front of the house the windows were exactly as they should be—black as the night sky. Diana and Clark were either asleep or still out.

It was time to get out, but Jeremy didn't let go.

"Don't be sad," he whispered in my ear. "Look at me."

I obeyed.

"You're too used to sacrificing for music," he said. "But we both want this, right?"

I gave him my best smile. *We can't have both!* I wanted to scream. *We can't both win!* Instead, I leaned forward and put my lips on his. This kiss was different from the first. Less startling. More aching. Less dreamlike. More desperate.

And when I left the cab this time, he was the one out of breath.

Chapter 12

told Heidi you'd be taking the next two weeks off," Diana informed me Monday morning when I came down to the kitchen table, French textbook in hand.

"What? Why?"

My question wasn't dignified with a response, unless a raised eyebrow over a sip of coffee counts. Diana had an unwritten *ask a stupid question, answer it yourself* policy.

I tossed my textbook on the counter. I needed to see Heidi, to talk her into being my alibi for Wednesday night.

Diana turned to the next page of the travel section of the *Tribune* and gestured to the stack of blueberry pancakes on the counter. "Clark was feeling domestic this morning."

I ignored the pancakes and poured myself a glass of orange juice. "But I might get behind . . ." I started feebly and then stopped.

"Carmen, are you kidding?"

It *was* a lame excuse. "I don't know. I guess."

"Let me remind you that you've got a full scholarship to Juilliard for this fall," she said, "which you'll hopefully be deferring. And besides, you've already completed your required courses. I'm glad you're enjoying physics and French, but you don't need them."

"What do you mean, deferring?"

She looked up over the rims of her reading glasses. "You know if you win the Guarneri you'll have performance obligations for the year. That's worth more than the prize money."

"Well, yeah," I said, unable to keep the annoyance out of my voice. "But I just assumed I'd be able to do both."

Diana sighed. "Life at Juilliard won't be like it is now. No Heidi, no days off. You'll have to go to classes."

"I know I'll have to go to classes. I'm not an idiot."

It had been like this since Saturday, with every interaction escalating from fine to furious in seconds.

The pile of things we were sitting on but not talking about—Inderal, Jeremy, her scary apology—was getting uncomfortable.

"You can see Heidi as soon as the Guarneri is over."

"But Heidi invited me to spend the night on Wednesday," I lied. Diana leaned back, folded her arms, and stared at me. Heidi's trendy Wicker Park apartment was slightly larger than a walk-in closet. And not only was it small, she had a roommate.

But it wasn't totally implausible. I'd spent a weekend sleeping on the floor, crammed between Heidi's bed and the bathroom door, last summer when Clark and Diana had gone to Montreal for their tenth anniversary. "Jenna's going out of town," I added. That wasn't unlikely either. Jenna, the roommate, was always traveling for work.

Diana opened her mouth, then hesitated. She was dying to say no, but couldn't. It was too much. I could see it in the way she had her arms folded and tucked around her, like they were holding her body together, and in the uneasiness around her eyes. I worried her. Good.

She shrugged. "That's fine. That's the night of the CSO function, so we won't be here anyway."

The fake indifference was stupid, but I didn't need to call her on it. I had to phone Heidi immediately. I picked up my French book and turned back to the stairs. "I'm going to go practice, I guess."

She didn't answer.

Heidi was surprisingly easy to convince. I'd expected her to turn responsible adult–like on me. We were only five years apart, but Diana's signature on her paycheck made her a slave to the grown-up code. Agreeing to be my alibi was a definite breach of that, but I'd underestimated her romantic side.

"Wait, wait, wait, tell it again," she'd said after I'd recounted the events of Friday night and then Sunday night, and then she screamed into the phone at the end of the story's second telling, just like she had on the first go round. "Of course you can spend the night!" she squealed. "But what are you going to wear?"

"I hadn't thought about it," I said, kicking off my shoes and climbing onto my bed.

"What is *wrong* with you? You haven't thought about it? Carmen, I've seen everything in your closet. You can't wear flannel pajama bottoms and a tank top to a Sox game with a guy," she said. "Or a performance gown."

She was right. There was a huge gap in my wardrobe between black tie and pajamas. It had almost killed me to put together something to wear on Sunday. I had jeans and T-shirts, but nothing especially cute.

"Don't worry. You can borrow something from me. When and where are you meeting him?"

"Five-thirty at the Drake," I said. "Or at Lavazza, actually."

"Lavazza?"

"It's an Italian coffee house beside the Drake, or under it. I'm not sure."

"Be at my place at two. I'll be your fairy godmother."

"Isn't that a little early?"

"Date prep takes time. Trust me."

"She'll probably call to check up on me," I warned.

"It's okay. I can lie."

"But what if she catches us?"

There was a pause on the other end of the phone. "She'll probably fire me."

I stopped. This wasn't fair. I shouldn't have asked her.

"It's okay, Carmen," she said softly. "It's almost over anyway. Juilliard in the fall, remember?"

I leaned back into my pillows and closed my eyes. I hadn't thought much about Juilliard—it was just the next logical career step—but then Diana had talked about deferring as if I'd already known and I'd wanted to throw my French textbook at her head.

"So you'll be here at two o'clock on Wednesday?" she asked.

"You're the best. Thanks."

"Don't thank me," she said. "Do you have any idea how long I've been waiting to give you a makeover?"

"I don't think that's a compliment. Should I be worried?"

"No, you should be excited."

I looked out the window, down to the street where the cab had pulled over and Jeremy had kissed me. And then where I'd kissed him. "I am."

I hung up and took a long look in the mirror. She'd been dying to give me a makeover?

I lifted my dark curly hair and twisted it up into a clip. I had Diana's eyes, grass green and almond shaped, but my nose was a little too big and my chin was a little too pointy. A makeover couldn't change that.

But Jeremy liked what he saw anyway, didn't he? I smiled. He did.

Unless he didn't. And suddenly there it was, Diana's voice in my head. *People will do anything to win . . .*

"Let's go over this again," Heidi said, running the wand through the lashes over my left eye. Her face was uncomfortably close. There was nowhere to look, so I was trying to focus on the crease between her nostril and her cheek rather than stare straight up her nose. "You meet him at five-thirty and take the Red Line to the stadium. The game is six-ten to—I don't know—nine-thirty? When does your mom's benefit dinner start?"

"Cocktails at eight, dinner at nine."

"Hmmm . . ." She put the mascara back on the table and reached for lipstick. "Dinner at nine and she's on the organizing committee?"

I nodded.

"Hey, did I give your permission to move your head?" She grabbed a tissue and wiped where the lipstick had smudged. "Benefit dinners go on forever. The earliest she could possibly be out of there is midnight, which means you have to be back here by then. You seriously ruined your lipline with the nodding."

"Midnight. I can do that, but I don't think she'll stop by. She's been really preoccupied with this dinner. It's been four days since the name Jeremy King was even spoken in our house. She thinks I believed her when she said he was just trying to mess with my brain before the competition."

Heidi bit her lip and squirted makeup remover on another tissue. "But you don't?"

"No. Not after going to that jazz club with him. Maybe I should be thinking about it though."

"It's kind of funny, actually," she said. "Most girls have to worry about guys just being after sex, but you should really be more worried if he isn't after sex. You just can't do anything normally, can you?"

I didn't answer. Sometimes Heidi's ability to hit the nail on the head hurt.

"What did you tell your mom, by the way? We should probably have our story straight."

"She thinks we're going to the game together."

She raised an eyebrow. "But I'm a Cubs fan."

"Yeah, but I needed to get the tickets from Clark somehow, and I'm pretty sure Diana doesn't keep track of the teams you cheer for."

"Well, I hope the Sox lose."

"That's fine with me, as long as I don't get busted."

"I'm glad I attacked those eyebrows the minute you walked in the door," she muttered, rubbing the sore skin above my eye with her thumb. "The redness is just now fading."

"I can do my own makeup you know."

"Wrong." She dipped a makeup brush in powder and swept it over my cheeks. "You never wear makeup unless you're on stage, and stage makeup makes you look like a transvestite."

"Thank you very much."

"You know what I mean. Just from up close."

I ran my hands over my straightened hair. It felt weird and smooth. "When do I get to look in the mirror?"

"When I'm done."

I fished my phone out of my purse. It was four fifty-one. "Hopefully that's soon. I need to go in ten minutes."

"Wrong again. You have to be late. Trust me, you

don't want to be there before he comes down. He needs to be standing around wondering if you're actually going to show up. It puts you in a position of power."

Power. I was so clueless. Obviously, there were mind game components to relationships I hadn't even begun to think through. I wasn't dumb enough to ask Heidi why it couldn't just be about me liking him and him liking me, but I could think it. "I'll be late then," I said.

"Good girl." Heidi took a bushy makeup brush off her desk, dipped it in a jar of bronzing powder, and gave my face a liberal dusting. Then she took two steps back and put her hands on her hips. "I give one freaking fantastic makeover. Put your boots on and stand up."

I zipped up the knee-high brown boots, stood, and adjusted the jean skirt. She squinted and grinned. "Go look in the mirror," she said, gesturing to the full length at the end of her very short hallway.

I turned and studied my reflection, slowly letting out the breath I hadn't even known I was holding. *Hallelujah, still me!* Somewhere midmakeover I'd started to worry that the finished product was going to look nothing like the original, and that Jeremy would take one look and know I'd spent the entire day primping. But Heidi *was* good. I looked fresh and natural, and my hair looked so . . . smooth. I ran my hands over it again. It was going to be hard to go back to the fuzzy ponytail.

Maybe I'd just never wash it again. Heidi's clothes certainly helped—Vera Wang flat boots, a snug indigo-denim mini, a vintage red wraparound sweater tied at my hip.

"Adorable. You look like Selena Gomez. And that skirt is perfect on you. It kind of makes me not want to wear it again," she said, as she slid a bracelet onto my arm. "What do you think?"

"I think you're a miracle worker."

"Hardly," she said, still grinning. "I had good raw material to work with."

"I love it. Thank you."

"Good. You can show your appreciation by not spilling mustard on the boots. They cost about half a month's rent." She fished around in her front closet and handed me a tailored khaki jacket. "You should go. You know which bus you're taking to the Drake?"

I nodded.

"And you'll be back . . ."

"By midnight," I said, and grabbed my purse from the couch.

"One more thing." She put her arm around my shoulder and walked me to the door. "Forget the violin crap and just have fun."

I gave her a hug. "I'll try."

* * *

The bus that took me from Heidi's to the Drake lurched and squealed like a drunk pig. My stop was still two away, but I stood and made my way to the exit, clinging to each safety bar as I went. I was starting to feel motion sick and Heidi was right. Being early would be a mistake.

I stepped off the bus and into a cloud of tulips. I'd forgotten about Tulip Days. Every April hundreds of thousands of tulips bloom overnight on Michigan Avenue. The explosion of crimson and tangerine was even more dizzying than the bus, a sea of rippling red heads bobbing around me.

I wove through clusters of shoppers and tulips, noting Diana's favorites as I passed them: Saks Fifth Avenue, La Perla, Tiffany & Co., Ralph Lauren, Gucci, Louis Vuitton—Michigan Avenue was high-end retail paradise.

Then up ahead the Gothic facade of Fourth Presbyterian Church appeared, and I remembered the hidden courtyard. I'd played concerts at the church before, but I'd never been there without my violin. Never alone.

I checked the time. It was 5:18 and the Drake was only a block up. I crossed over and slipped under the graceful stone archway that led into the courtyard. It was empty. Stillness weighted the air. I walked slowly to the fountain and surveyed the space around me. Emerald green ivy blanketed the stone walls, growing up to the sky. It looked so vibrant I reached out and touched a leaf with my fingers. It was warm from the sun. That ivy worked a kind of magic on my nerves, absorbing the sounds of traffic and shoppers on the other side of the wall. Just a few feet away, they didn't exist.

My purse buzzed, bringing me back. *Don't be Jeremy*, I prayed. *Don't be calling to cancel.* I dug for my phone and raced to come up with a response for if he was and how to sound completely indifferent about it, or maybe even beat him to it and cancel first. My finger was on the talk button, ready to press it, when I glanced down at the screen.

Diana's cell.

I exhaled shakily.

It could be worse. I could already be at the game. If I was with Jeremy, he'd hear me lying to my mother and start wondering why he was hanging out with a twelve-year-old. The phone buzzed again. What would I say if she wanted to talk to Heidi? *She's in the bathroom.* And what if she wanted to stop by for some reason on her way to the benefit? *We're on our way out for dinner.* Maybe. It buzzed again. Next time it would go to voicemail. That could worry her enough to send her straight to Heidi's. I pressed talk.

"Hi." My voice was at least two whole tones higher than normal.

"Having fun?" she asked.

"Yeah."

"Good. What exactly are you two planning on for tonight?"

"Dinner, then the game."

"Great. Can I talk to Heidi for a sec?"

My heart thumped. I took a deep breath. "Uh, she's in the bathroom."

There was a short pause then in the same careless voice, "Is that why she can't talk? Or is it because she's in her apartment and you're nowhere near there?"

In all my musing on the nature of God, on whether He existed or not, I sometimes forgot there was another option: *Diana was God.* How else could she be so freaking omniscient?

"I'm assuming Heidi coached you on the bathroom excuse since that's exactly where she said *you* were when I called her apartment a minute ago."

I groaned. Heidi hadn't even coached me on the excuse! Why was it so hard for her to believe I thought for myself occasionally?

"Where are you?" The tone was all business.

I looked up at the web of ivy. Early evening sun had warmed the stone beneath it to a pinkish brown. Had she already squeezed the answer out of Heidi? "Church," I answered.

"*What?*"

She would be picturing Saint Clements Holy Catholic Church, the church we faithfully ignored fifty Sundays of the year. (Face time on Easter and Christmas seemed like plenty.) Why correct her?

"Why would you be at church? Am I really supposed to believe that? Are you with Jeremy King?"

If Heidi had told her I was seeing Jeremy, lying would be pointless. She might be trying to trap me. But I wasn't with Jeremy. Yet.

"No."

"I don't believe you. And you're sure as hell not at church either. What are you thinking, Carmen?" Her voice cracked over my name. She waited, though the question was obviously rhetorical. What I was thinking had certainly never been of any interest to her before. When she continued, her voice was quiet again, but still just as agitated. "I thought you understood our discussion about Jeremy's motives. I guess I was wrong."

"You *were* wrong," I said, "but not about me. About him." Whose voice was that? She sounded like me, but with a spine.

I could just picture Diana's little nostrils flaring. "If you're going to disregard my advice as your mother that's fine, but as your manager, I'm ordering you to stop being an idiot and get home."

Or else? The absence of a threat was insulting. Was I

supposed to obey just because she was angry and because I always did what I was told?

My eyes followed a shoot of ivy as it twisted and climbed skyward over the stones. I could call Jeremy and make up an excuse. Or tell him the truth. At that point, it wouldn't matter. I could walk out to Michigan Avenue, hail a cab and be home in fifteen minutes, practice an hour or two, and be in bed by nine.

"I don't think so," I said.

"*Carmen*—"

"No. I've got plans. I'll be back at Heidi's around midnight, and I'll be home tomorrow morning."

I hung up before I had the chance to hear her response. I powered off my phone.

Chapter 13

was starting to worry." Jeremy grinned and leaned back in his chair under the red Lavazza umbrella. He didn't look worried. His hair was wind whipped, and his sleeves were pushed up. In front of him sat a glass, empty except for a small chocolate puddle at the bottom, atop a half-finished crossword puzzle. "I'm falling in love with this place," he said, and gestured back toward the shop.

Along with a jewelry store and a handful of expensive boutiques, Lavazza sat beneath the hotel lobby, opening onto the street. Behind Jeremy, the Drake's awning fluttered and a doorman stood sentinel by glass rotating doors.

"My grandparents stay at the Drake when they come to Chicago," I said. "I've eaten at the restaurant inside but never here before." I looked through the window at the tubs of glossy gelato, and pretended not to notice that he was staring at me.

"Sorbetto cremespresso," he said and tapped his pencil against the empty glass. "I'm addicted. It's probably just melted coffee ice cream, but they can charge double with a name like that." He stood and slid the pencil into his back pocket. He looked good in jeans and a rugby shirt, long and muscular.

"You look different," he said, squinting.

The un-compliment. My least favorite. "Thanks. I've always wanted to be told I looked different. Are you ready to go?"

"Your hair," he said. "It's straight."

I shrugged. "Sometimes I straighten it." He didn't need to know that the first of those sometimes was today. I checked the V-neck of my sweater to make sure my bra wasn't showing, feeling suddenly like a Barbie doll someone else had dressed up.

"So how do we get there?" he asked.

"The Red Line."

"Lead the way," he said, tossing his crossword puzzle into the pile of café newspapers.

We walked side by side, but at completely different

gaits, my legs taking three steps for every two of his. He didn't seem to notice.

"So, have you been pretty busy the last couple of days?" I said. Ouch, that sounded desperate. Why hadn't I just lead with, *Why haven't you called me?*

He shrugged.

With all the anticipation, and Heidi's primping, and replaying the first kiss and then the second kiss every ten minutes for the last few days, I hadn't planned for awkwardness. That was dumb. I should have been writing up and memorizing lists of potential conversation topics.

I shouldn't have flushed all my Inderal. If I could take just one, this jittery feeling in my gut would be gone.

I glanced over at him. His hands were in his pockets and he was whistling something familiar. Maybe the awkwardness was only in my head. I leaned in to hear the tune.

"Brahms Sonata in G Major," I said, finally recognizing it. "Is that part of your semifinals program?"

He stopped whistling. "I don't want to talk violin."

Nope. Awkwardness not just in my head. We reached the corner and waited with the other pedestrians to cross. Abruptly, he turned to me and I saw the angry red line on the left side of his jaw from practicing. It looked sore.

"Sorry," he said. "I'm just stressed out." Then he gave a half shrug/half grin. "Let's just have fun tonight."

"Sure."

We crossed the street and climbed the stairs to the train platform where a crowd of wound-up White Sox fans had gathered, shaking big foam fingers, already smelling like beer in their pinstripe jerseys. Poor Clark. I pictured him at a table with a bunch of symphony lovers trying to nod his way through dinner without falling asleep.

Jeremy looked around at the people on the platform. "I can't believe I'm finally going to my first baseball match."

"Yeah, we call them games here."

"Whatever. To be honest, I'm not even a hundred percent on all the rules."

"It's pretty simple," I said, but then wondered if it was, or if I'd just always known the rules of baseball. "So, do baseball fans look like soccer fans?" I asked.

"More or less," he said. "Except we call it football there, and I'm not afraid for my life, like I would be in a crowd of Manchester United fans."

"That wild?"

"In a crazy, lawless, we'll-kill-you-and-eat-you-for-sport-if-you're-cheering-for-the-wrong-team sort of a way. Who are the White Sox playing, by the way?"

"Minnesota Twins."

"Twins? That seems like a really lame name for a sports team."

"I agree. The fact that you recognize that means you're going to be a great White Sox fan."

When the train came the whole crowd packed into the cars, and I found myself wedged between Jeremy's body and a greasy window. We were too close to talk, what with my head being a full foot below his, but that was kind of a relief. The nearest pole was too far away to hold onto, so when the train lurched forward, I fell into him, my face landing in his chest. He laughed and caught me, then helped me regain my balance, but left his hand resting on my lower back. His shirt smelled fresh and sweet like detergent.

We arrived in time to see the end of batting practice, which Clark was always adamant about. That and staying until the last out. None of that leaving-early-to-beat-the-crowds crap.

"Who's throwing the opening pitch?" Jeremy asked.

"A fellow Brit, I believe. And a musician too."

"Should I guess?"

"Yeah."

"Um, Elton John?"

"No. Younger and less pudgy," I said.

"I hope you don't think Madonna is actually British."

"Nope, but I think *she* thinks she's British. It isn't her anyway."

"I give up," he said.

"Victoria Beckham."

"Of course. Our nation's greatest asset. I don't know if I'd actually consider her a musician."

"Me neither. How about an actress? I think the Spice Girls may have made a movie."

Just then she tottered out with five-inch heel/running shoe hybrids on her feet, looking like an anorexic bird on stilts. She gave the crowd the peace sign, and tossed the ball a couple of feet. Everyone, including Jeremy and me, went crazy.

The game started, and in the mayhem of the screaming fans, we slipped back into what we had been at the jazz club. We watched the game, or pretended to watch the game, but really just watched each other, and talked, and felt the spaces between us shrink.

At the top of the third he went to get food and came back from concessions with two sausage dogs covered in grilled onions and peppers so hot my lips burned. We ate them while making fun of the of the Kissing Cam victims, cheering especially hard for the holdouts when they finally gave in and kissed.

Between the third and fourth he helped me compose a haiku about the Minnesota Twins (Ball-dropping fat dudes/ Your mothers have moustaches/Girl Scouts run faster). When we scored our only run in the seventh, I spilled my soda all over his pants, but he just laughed and bought me another one.

All in all, it was perfect.

"This feeling crosses the cultural divide," Jeremy said

as we watched the final pitches being hurled. "It doesn't even matter that I've only been a Sox fan for a few hours. I want to throw a peanut at that idiot in the Twins jersey over there who won't shut up."

"Agreed."

"You think I should do it?"

"I was agreeing with the feeling. I'd rather you didn't get us thrown out of the game."

"For you," he said and rolled over the top of the paper bag of peanuts, then put it on my lap.

Losing the game didn't even feel all that bad. There was an understanding among the fans that it was more noble to love a team with heart than a blood-sucking soulless franchise like the Twins.

Clark would be checking the score and swearing into his cocktail.

The entire stadium seemed to stand and push toward the exits simultaneously, but we sat still, neither of us ready for it to be over.

"Should we go?" Jeremy asked finally. People in the aisles were still just inching toward the bottle-necked exit.

"Let's wait."

"I guess it's not like they're going anywhere fast."

"Nope," I said. "Your jeans still wet?"

He pressed his hand to his thigh where I'd spilled the Coke. "Yeah."

"Sorry."

"You don't need to apologize again. I probably deserved it."

"For what?"

"I don't know. The last obnoxious thing I said?"

I thought for a moment. "You haven't really said anything obnoxious since we got here." He hadn't said a word about violin either. Not one.

He laughed. "You sound surprised."

"I guess I am. Would you like me to count it against one of the obnoxious things you said when I first met you?"

"That would be great." He looked like he wanted to say more, like he wanted to apologize for that ugly competitive streak he'd let show. But neither of us wanted that. We were in a perfect bubble of baseball and drunk Sox fans and mindless banter. No need to ruin it now.

He stood and offered me his hand. I took it and he pulled me up, then turned and led me out of the stadium.

"What time do you have to be home by?" he asked as we stepped away from the doors and into the dark. A stream of people flowed past us to the train platform.

"I'm not going home. I'm spending the night at a friend's, but I'm supposed to be back there at midnight." For all I knew, Diana was already waiting for me on Heidi's couch. But I wasn't going back yet. She was going to kill me whether I saw her in ten minutes or in ten hours.

"Hmmm." Jeremy looked down at me and smiled with one corner of his mouth. "Staying at a friend's? So that's how you're dealing with the leash?"

"Don't judge me. Your parents let you go halfway across the world by yourself and stay there for weeks on end. I'm not allowed to go to the bathroom without permission. Trust me, you'd lie too."

"It's not as wonderful as you think it is," he said. "Being on my own, I mean. My mom has to stay at home with my brother. He's disabled and it's tricky to work out care for anything longer than a couple of days. And my dad. He's . . . high stress. I'm on my own because I have to be if I want to do violin."

"Sorry."

"Don't be sorry," he said. "You obviously don't have it easy either."

A wind blew into us and through Heidi's thin jacket. I shivered.

"I'd offer you a jacket, but I don't have one," he said.

"And I'm already wearing one."

"That too. Not to mention the fact that you still have the sweater I gave you on Sunday."

"Oops. I was going to bring that." That was a complete lie. I didn't ever want to have to part with that sweater.

He paused and ran a hand through his hair. His expression changed as he clenched his jaw, and his fingers tapped nervously against his jeans. He was mulling over something. "I've got something I want to show you."

"Sure, go ahead."

"No, it's not here. It's back at the hotel."

"What is it?"

"I can't tell you. You just have to see it."

Possibilities. I looked back toward the stadium. The artificial lights had given everything a Hollywood glow; there'd been warmth in the rich colors. But we'd left. Out here, things were real again.

"All right," I said.

The trip back was nothing like the first ride. We got seats and he stared out the window at the murky outlines as they flew by in the dark. I listened to two older men a couple of rows up blame the loss on a fourth inning call the umpire had screwed up. In their drunken opinions, that had been the turning point.

"Why didn't you come hear me on Saturday?" The question was out before I remembered we weren't talking about violin.

He looked uncomfortable. "I . . ."

"No. You don't have to answer."

"Yes, I do. I couldn't." He folded his arms over his chest. "It's too close to the Guarneri. I can't listen to other violinists and not go a little crazy. I don't need to hear how amazing your Tchaikovsky is right now."

"But you don't know it's amazing."

He smirked. "I'm sure. The competitions, the recordings, the Grammy—that's all just hype? I have to make a conscious effort not to think about you already when I'm performing. I don't need more stress added to it."

"But you seem so in love with your *own* music on stage." I didn't say *in love with yourself*, but it hung in the air between us.

"You're dancing around calling me a narcissist onstage, but nobody wants to see a self-conscious violinist out there. Especially not a guy."

"I don't see what gender has to do with it."

"*You* can go out and be shy or nervous, and you're beautiful so the audience thinks you're sweet and lovely and whatever else. If I pulled that, the review in the paper would describe me as tense or incompetent. That doesn't sell tickets."

"So much for not talking about violin."

"I guess that's impossible," he said, his voice resolved and a little sad. He took my hand again, this time lacing his fingers through mine. "I'm sorry I didn't go to your concert."

"Don't be sorry. I kind of wish I hadn't gone to yours, except for all the stuff that happened afterward."

"So why did you come?" he asked.

"Um . . ." Why didn't I have a simple answer to that question? Enough people had asked me—Heidi, Diana, now Jeremy. "Because . . ." I looked around the train at the people laughing and shouting. They looked like they'd forgotten we'd lost.

"You look like you're hoping someone will give you the right answer."

"I wish. There is no right answer."

"Try the truth."

"I came because you didn't make any sense to me," I said.

He waited for more.

"From everything I'd read, you were *me*. A British, male version of *me*. And then when I saw you that day from the Rhapsody patio . . ."

"When you were spying."

"Can we call it researching, please? When I saw you, the curiosity just got bigger. I've always felt like, I don't know, like the only one of my species, I guess. But then there you were, a version of me, and I wanted to see how you did it, if you knew how to age out of being a child prodigy. I'm kind of botching it at the moment."

He was silent.

Was I making any sense at all? Probably not, but I babbled on anyway. "I'm just pissing off my teacher, pissing off my mom, pissing off myself. . . . I miss performing and being happy with it, not having to be mad at myself about every little thing that didn't go perfectly."

"So, now that you know me, does it look like I'm doing it right?"

"What do you mean?"

"From your vantage point, am I leaving child-prodigy-land properly, or am I botching it too?"

I looked into his eyes. "I guess I can't tell. But I was wrong. We aren't the same. You're isolated. I hate being smothered and pressured, but I'm not alone. You are."

He flinched.

"I'm sorry. I shouldn't have said that."

"No, you're right."

And then there were the differences I couldn't say aloud. I was insecure, but he had a cockiness to him that took hours to wear down. And he didn't have the Inderal problem. I wasn't fooling myself about Inderal. One performance without it didn't equate to complete independence. It was what it was—one tiny victory. Just the beginning.

"I don't know," I said. "We're too different to compare."

He nodded.

"So now that we've smashed through the no-violin-talk rule, what's the Menuhin school like?" I already knew it was incredibly competitive and arguably the best music high school in the world, for violinists especially. I would've loved to have gone there, but Diana would never have let me go to a boarding school, especially not on the other side of the world. I still didn't know what she was going to do when I went to Juilliard in the fall. Move to New York, probably. It was weird that she hadn't brought it up, but maybe she was counting on winning the Guarneri and having me defer for a year.

Jeremy stretched his arms over his head. "School is . . ." He stopped to think. "Intense. It's kind of nice being away from it all for a while. I'm learning a lot there, but just walking down the practice room hall, you can feel the pressure. It's everywhere. There's just this insane amount of talent and ambition in the air, which means everyone is always on edge, you know? It makes me a bit frantic, actually. And we all know that it only takes one day of not playing your best and there are twenty other violinists snapping at your heels, ready to take your chair in orchestra, or your scholarship, or whatever. And since it's a boarding school, there's no forgetting it, no escaping to your family, or at least not for me. Mine live in Leeds, which is a good three and a half hours north of Surrey."

"Do you miss them?"

"I don't think about it. I spend some weekends with my grandma at her house down south. She lives right on the beach, in a cottage on the English Channel."

"That sounds nice."

He smiled. "It is. Charminster. That's the name of the town Gigi lives near."

"Gigi? That's a cute nickname for a grandma."

"Her real name is Georgianna. Anyway, so I'm not *entirely* alone . . ."

"I shouldn't have said that. It's not really what I meant. I—"

"It's okay, Carmen." He put his hand on mine.

"This next one is our stop," I said, and stood up.

We walked in silence from the station to the hotel. What did he want to show me? It had to be violin related. Maybe he had some incredible new instrument or some huge Guarneri secret or . . . what?

Of course, there was the other option. In the movies and on TV, *come back to my hotel with me* always means sex. But it couldn't be that. Diana would roll her eyes and say I was so naïve—not out of concern for my innocence, but because sleeping with Jeremy would make me so much more vulnerable than I already was. It would put my raw little heart in the palm of his hand.

I pumped my cold hands and folded my arms across

my chest to warm myself. I hated that she'd put that idea into my brain.

But would it be so bad if sex was what he really wanted? Couldn't I forget that he was Jeremy King for just one night and worry about the aftermath later? It seemed like a small price for one perfect piece of normalcy— heartbreak later for happiness now. And if I acknowledged that a betrayal of some kind was probably coming, maybe that would free me to do what I wanted tonight. Maybe.

"Home, sweet home," Jeremy said, and looked up. The Drake shone like a crystal-studded pillar, lights glittering from the windows. The doorman nodded as he opened the door for us, and Jeremy gave him a familiar, "Hey." After weeks at the Drake, he was probably friends with the entire staff.

I'd forgotten the elegance of the entrance hall, the flowers, the chandeliers, the lagoon blue carpets. I paused at the bottom of the grand staircase that led to the lobby, a warning sounding in my head. I shouldn't be here.

Jeremy looked back over his shoulder. "Coming?" he asked. I followed.

The cold air that clung to our bodies was gone by the time we reached the top step. We passed through the lobby, by the front desk and the concierge, past the couches where two gowned women perched beside tuxedoed men, and through to the elevators. Jeremy pressed the up button. We waited. Why did I feel so out of breath?

He had a large corner suite on the tenth floor with the same lagoon blue carpets, a white king-size bed, mahogany desks and tables, and a stiff-looking couch. It looked gently messed—a sweater on the couch, a pile of books beside his bed, a portable metal music stand, extended to its full height and sagging under the weight of several books of music—but not a complete disaster, and not sterile and hotel-ish either. His violin and bow were out of the case, lying perpendicular on the bed, a dark cross over the bone white silk of the comforter.

"Your violin," I said.

"What about it?"

"It's beautiful. So different close up." The wood was the color of black coffee, but without the stage lights its gloss was gone. The color was warmer than I'd remembered, like a layer of red ran underneath.

"It's no Strad," he said, tossing the key card on the credenza.

Was that an edge to his voice? Maybe not.

"The color, I mean. Mine's quite orange. Do you mind?" I asked and walked toward the bed.

"Go ahead."

I so rarely picked up anyone else's instrument. Yuri didn't take his out of the case to teach anymore. When I was little he'd had it out for every lesson, preferring to demonstrate rather than make the translation from music to Ukrainian to English. Yuri's violin was the color of hay, the color of Jeremy's hair.

I picked it up by the neck and placed it on my shoulder. Everything was the same and everything was different. The wood of the neck felt smoother, and maybe a hair wider than mine. The space for my thumb between the frog and the wrap of the bow was tighter. I played a few notes, the opening phrase of my favorite Bach Partita. The tone was bright and beautiful, but not deep. I tested out the lower register, and then moved up the instrument until I was playing the high notes on the E string. He was right. It was no Strad, but the sound was sweet and the instrument was responsive.

Jeremy sat watching me from the armchair beside the TV, leaning back, arms folded.

"Nice," I said.

He shrugged. I stared back, but he had an intensity that held his features perfectly still and I looked away first. He probably thought I'd picked it up just so I could feel better about my violin. Now a compliment would sound fake, and anything less was rude. I shouldn't have asked to play it.

"It is nice," he said. "My parents took out a second mortgage on their house to finance it. But it's not . . . Well, you know."

It wasn't the kind of instrument he deserved. Again, I

thought of him on stage. No, not at all what he deserved.

"I get funding from Arts Council England, and there's money from CD sales and competitions for travel, but not enough for what I really need. That's why I have to win," he said.

Of course. He needed the violin. Four years with a Guarneri violin was a long time. Long enough to make a lot of money, long enough to find a patron to set him up with another instrument.

"You look surprised," he said.

"No. Not surprised," I faltered, realizing too late that I was saying the wrong thing. "I just sometimes forget about that part of the prize."

"If I had a Strad I wouldn't be fighting to get my hands on a Guarneri either."

I put his violin back on the bed, laying the bow beside it, and sat down on the couch across from him. It was just as stiff as it looked. I shouldn't have come up. It seemed ridiculous now, the very idea that he'd had sex on his mind when he asked me here. Violin was clearly the only thing either of us could think about right now.

"What did you want to show me?" I asked.

"Two things. The first was my violin. The second"—he stood, walked toward the bed as he spoke—"is this picture." He pulled a photo in a silver frame from the nightstand and passed it to me.

Three people stood posed at the edge of what looked like a farmer's market. Crates of carrots, tomatoes, and eggplant cluttered a fruit and vegetable stand behind them, larger boxes of produce were wedged between the legs of the table on the cobblestone beneath. On the left stood a drained-looking woman, tall and thin with wispy blond hair and skin so pale you could see veins at her temples. She seemed old, but when I examined her features, I could see she wasn't. She just looked tired.

On the far right, Jeremy leaned against the corner of the table, arms crossed, looking like a younger, hardier version of the woman. Same blond hair and slender body, but with muscle and blood under his tanned skin. The picture must have been taken recently because he was the Jeremy I recognized now, not the boy from the picture in the Carnegie Hall program.

Between them a boy sat in a wheelchair. The chair was angled away from the camera, but the boy's head was turned and he stared directly into the lens. Reddish hair blew across his face, partially covering his eyes. He had the woman's pale skin, but Jeremy's jaw and his same determined glare.

"Your brother?"

"Yeah." Jeremy said.

"And your mom?"

"Uh-huh."

"How old is your brother?" His features looked boyish, but his limbs were long.

"Thirteen."

"My mum has a huge garden," he explained. "It's a hobby, but she takes it pretty seriously. She spends every spare second in it, actually. The picture is taken at a produce market in Leeds. That's where I live, or they live, I should say. I don't even know where I live. Surrey, I guess."

"And your brother, has he always been in a wheelchair?"

"No. He was diagnosed with muscular dystrophy when he was four, but he didn't need a wheelchair until last year. That's what happens with muscular dystrophy. Slowly. Everything gets worse."

I stared at the boy in the picture again, and this time saw his slouch and the way his hands curled up in his lap.

"How slowly?" The second the words were out, I wished I could suck them back in.

"Do you mean, when will he die?"

I didn't say anything, just stared at the picture: the woman's weary expression, the boy's defiant stare, Jeremy's athletic frame, then back to the woman again. I looked up at Jeremy and nodded. He seemed so matter-of-fact, so casual. Arms still crossed behind his head, he was watching the slow twirl of the ceiling fan.

His voice had produced the words in the same tone that he'd ordered me another soda with just a couple of hours ago.

"The doctors don't know or won't say. Nobody will, or at least not to me. Robbie's case is aggressive. That's his name, Robbie. From what I've read and overheard, it'll be within the year or so, but that's just what I'm getting from my own random Google searches and conversations between my parents that I'm not supposed to hear. Nobody talks to me about any of it."

"That sucks," I said. What a lame comment. But what was I supposed to say? Maybe nothing at all.

"I have to win, Carmen."

Out of nowhere. We sat in silence, his comment burning the space between us. My ears felt hot, my face felt hot.

"I have to win," he repeated, "for Robbie. It's the only big thing I can do for him. I don't know how much longer he's even going to be able to hear me—" His voice cracked and he looked down at his hands, spreading the fingers as wide as he could in front of him. His face had that look that people have when they are trying not to cry, nostrils wide, eyes glassy, chin pulled in. "You're the only one who can beat me. I need you to let me win."

I heard, but I didn't hear. The words were too improbable to digest. But then my brain repeated them and my stomach dropped. I felt sick. "That . . ."

"Carmen. *Please*."

"That's not fair. You can't ask that."

"Not fair? Fair is meaningless." His voice was so pleading. "I think about what's not fair every single time I look at my brother. Every time I think that in five years I'll be in school or onstage and he won't be *anything* or *anywhere*. Nothing is fair. Sometimes things are a little *less* unfair. That's it. That's as close to fair as life gets."

"It's not something you can ask, though." I stopped for breath. I had to get control and think, but I felt so flustered. "This is my dream too, Jeremy. I shouldn't have to explain what I've sacrificed to you of all people, and I know that sounds like nothing compared to why you need to win, compared to your brother, but . . ."

"But you could win the next Guarneri! Robbie doesn't have four years!"

"I . . ."

"Just think about it. That's all I'm asking, and I wouldn't even be doing that if I didn't think you were the kind of person who would consider it. If I didn't . . ." He hesitated and pushed his hair out of his eyes, looking miserable. "I feel like I know your heart, Carmen."

I was such an idiot. Diana had been right, or at least close enough. He wasn't trying to break my heart, but he certainly wasn't falling in *love* with me. Just thinking the word, realizing how stupid it was to have believed that he felt that way made my insides hurt, made me want to melt into the couch and disappear completely. I stood up and walked over to the glass door. It opened up onto a balcony, but I didn't go out. Instead I leaned my forehead into the glass, letting the cold flow into me.

Jeremy was trying to win my love or friendship or whatever this was, so he could *appeal* to my heart, and if it got broken in the process, that was just collateral damage. But using his dying brother to guilt me into throwing the competition—that couldn't really be what he was doing, could it? He had to know his winning wouldn't fix his brother. Or maybe he'd convinced himself it would.

Diana may have been only half right about Jeremy, but she was completely right about me. I was naïve. I kept my forehead to the glass and brought my fingers trembling up to press against the cool surface. My body ached for Inderal. Or was it my heart that needed numbing? Why had I flushed them all? Just one was all I needed. Just one.

Lake Michigan was black under the starlit sky.

I had to ask, but it was easier if I didn't look at him. "Is that why you kissed me?"

The minute the words were out, I knew the answer. I hadn't needed to ask.

The pause was a little too long. "Of course not."

"Yes, it is." My voice was shaking but I couldn't steady it. "That's why you wanted to meet me, why you played *Carmen Fantasy* for your encore, why you pretended to like me and told me I was beautiful. It was part of some big soften-Carmen-up plan so you could convince me to just give you the Guarneri competition!"

"Carmen, that's ridiculous."

"Really? I don't think so." My brain hurt as it tripped over his words again and again. Something didn't make sense. "What makes you even think I could beat you? You *know* you're the one who everyone is expecting to win. You've never even heard me play!"

"I lied," Jeremy said softly. "I went to your concert on Saturday."

I pulled my head from the glass and turned to him. "What? Why did you tell me you didn't go?"

He stood slowly and took a step toward me, then stopped. "I didn't want you to know how freaked out I was. I liked you, *still* like you. I'd just kissed you the night before—see? That was before I heard you, before I knew how . . . how . . ."

I thought back to Saturday. The horror of the anxiety without Inderal, the vomiting, the fight with Diana. I should have crumbled on stage and humiliated myself. But I hadn't. The performance had been magical. The way everything fit so perfectly together, every movement and emotion, it had felt so incredible.

"You were amazing," he said. "I don't think I can beat you."

His shoulders sagged under the weight of his words. I had felt the same way when I heard him play.

"I shouldn't have asked you," he said, eyes lowered. "You're right. It isn't fair." He stood frozen in the center of the room, wanting to come to me, I could tell, but not sure what I'd do. Finally, he looked up and something about those beautiful blue eyes made the humiliation explode inside of me.

I stepped back, almost tripping over my own feet. "I have to go."

He reached out and grabbed my hand. "Don't," he said, and I saw raw desperation in his face. He knew he was losing.

"Don't touch me!" I shook his hand loose. I spun around and ran for the door.

"Carmen, wait . . ." I heard him call into the hall before it clanged shut behind me, but he was too late. He'd already lost.

Chapter 14

Diana wasn't waiting for me at Heidi's apartment like I thought she would be. Instead, I found Heidi alone, sitting cross-legged on her countertop, eating warm brownies out of the pan with a soup spoon, a scared-rabbit look in her eye. Diana hadn't called Heidi back after she'd spoken to me, and their first conversation had ended with Diana calling Heidi a liar and hanging up on her. I spent half the night reassuring her that everything was going to be fine, which we both knew was a lie, and then the second half tossing and turning on Jenna's lumpy futon, waiting for Diana to show up and drag me home by the hair. It was masterful on her part.

She must have known the anticipation would be brutal. I left the next morning exhausted, with a headache and a thorny ball of dread in my stomach. It felt like I'd swallowed a ball of tinfoil.

When I got home Diana said almost nothing to me, which was, again, masterful. Bracing for a verbal onslaught was so much worse than just plain getting yelled at. There was a slight glimmer of hostility in her eye when she nodded hello, but that was it.

Confused, I did the only thing that made sense. I hid in my room.

Diana ignored me, but she finally did phone Heidi later that day. I had a fairly good listening spot, perched on the top step, just outside my room. I sat rubbing my calves nervously and waiting for her to drop the sugary tone and lose it on Heidi. She didn't.

French and physics were discontinued—"Carmen has already completed the courses she needs for graduation and we need to eliminate distractions right now"—a vague invitation was issued—"Don't let this incident keep you from feeling comfortable as a visitor. You've been such an important part of Carmen's development, please come see her anytime. But do call first"— and of course career advice was dispensed—"Can I make a little unsolicited suggestion, Heidi? Go get some training in something more marketable. Have you ever considered becoming a paralegal?"

Once I'd been ignored long enough, restrictions were put in place. Lockdown measures were pretty severe. I was allowed to go to the bathroom. I was allowed to practice, sleep, and read. I was allowed to fix myself something to eat. That was about it. Everything else required permission and/or a chaperone. Iron fists, it turned out, come in all shapes and sizes. This one had a French manicure.

Diana may have been all poise and control on the outside, but I could see something else beneath. She was a mess inside. She was practically vibrating, the stress beneath her skin giving her a frantic glow. It was strangely satisfying to know it was all because of me. *I* was the catalyst for every nerve-twisting headache she suffered, and she did a terrible job of hiding it. Her mind was ticking like one of those game show wheels with spokes that clicked as the wheel spun, and each click was Carmen-related: keep Carmen from freaking out, keep Carmen away from Jeremy, get Carmen to her lesson, convince Carmen to take her meds, make Carmen listen to Yuri, keep Carmen from freaking out, pretend I'm not freaking out so Carmen won't freak out, and so on.

The power was a nice surprise, like finding a candy in your pocket while waiting for the El in a snowstorm. It was still freezing, but at least I had something sweet to suck on. She could ground me until I was thirty, but I still was the one in control.

I wasn't nice enough to tell her she was worrying about the wrong things. I wasn't going to freak out. Semifinals were in five days, finals were in eight. I had more important things to worry about than how close to the edge I could push Diana. Like the look on Robbie's face in that photograph, sad but willful, or the way Jeremy's shoulders had slumped and his eyes had refused to meet mine after I'd said no.

I'd said no. I'd meant it. What he'd asked was unreasonable, unfair, insulting, ridiculous. . . .

But none of that made me feel less guilty, or less used. Why had I actually believed he liked me? Diana had warned me. I should have listened. I just hadn't wanted to believe her. And maybe if I was a better person I would have considered his request for longer than a second.

Apparently, I couldn't even be trusted to take the train to my lesson. Clark offered to drive me with all the subtlety of a sumo wrestler in ballet shoes.

"Um, I have to go up to the office anyway, and that's good because you won't get cold, right?" he said, and took my violin case right off my shoulder.

I almost pointed out that it was warm outside and Yuri's apartment was in the opposite direction from his office, but why bother? My problem wasn't with Clark. It wasn't like being my prison guard was his idea. "Sure, I just have to get my music from upstairs."

"Hurry. I've got a ten o'clock meeting."

I checked my watch. There was no way he'd be on time after driving me out to Yuri's. Diana must not have given him a choice.

I ran up both flights of stairs, two steps at a time.

"Slow down!" Diana's voice called from her room. "Are you *trying* to fall and break your arm?" I didn't answer. I did speed up though.

My music was on the stand where I'd left it. I paused to look down to where Clark was loading my violin into his trunk. The case was strong enough to withstand being run over by a semi, but he always handled it like it was a live bomb that might detonate at any moment. He shut the trunk, then walked around to the passenger side of the car, opened the door, and put what looked like a paper bag on my seat. I was too far away to tell for sure.

I ran back down the stairs, jumping three at a time, but Diana wouldn't give me the satisfaction of yelling at me to slow down so I could ignore her again.

"What's this?" I asked, picking the brown bag off the passenger seat and sliding into the car.

Clark just smiled and put the car into gear.

I looked inside. It was a little piece of sympathy, a secret gift between fellow hostages—a glazed doughnut.

Tears welled up behind my eyes. It was easy to keep it

together when I was at war with the whole world. Yuri, Jeremy, Diana—they couldn't make me cry. But Clark . . . I suddenly wished I was going anywhere in the world except my lesson. "You're the best," I said, peeling off the wax paper it was stuck to and taking a bite.

"Sure."

I had every reason to dread this lesson. Things with Yuri were going to be sticky.

First, there was the way my last lesson had ended— he'd practically thrown me out. And then I'd turned it all musically upside down on Saturday night by ignoring everything he'd been yelling at me to do for the last year. He was going to be livid about that. It wouldn't matter that I'd given an exciting performance for the first time in a long time. In fact, that might make him even angrier, like I was tossing the things he taught me back in his face.

I didn't want to think about the other possibility, the one even worse than him being angry. He might be completely indifferent. Detached.

I passed through the parade of food smells in Yuri's apartment building, wishing I had somewhere to wash the sugary doughnut glaze from my hands.

His door was cracked open, just an inch. It was never open.

"Hi," I called and walked in, then closed the door behind me.

The door to his studio was open too. He sat at his studio desk, pipe in his mouth, already puffing.

"Can I wash my hands?" I didn't wait for an answer, just wandered around the mismatched furniture and piles of clutter to the kitchen sink, where I had to move aside a small mountain of dirty sauce pans just to reach the faucet. The water in this building took forever to warm up from ice cold, so I didn't bother waiting.

"Did you know your door was open?" I asked, walking through the open doorway and into his studio. I put my case down on the chair.

Yuri blinked. "Open?" He looked completely bewildered. "Must have forgot."

Most of the time Yuri seemed beyond age, so old he was timeless. But then he'd do something little, like leave his precious lock undone, his door open, and I'd see frailty. He was ninety-two. That was nearly a century. What if he was losing his mind?

"What are you staring at?" he said, pulling the pipe from his veiny blue lips.

Nope. Still himself.

"Nothing." I started to unzip my case, but he held up a hand.

"Not today."

I focused my eyes over his head out the window, bracing myself. He didn't even want me to take my violin out—this was going to be bad.

"Sit," he said.

I moved my case off the leather chair and lowered myself into it. It felt stiff. I could only remember sitting in it once before. I'd had mono and was feeling light-headed in the middle of the lesson, and maybe one other time when . . . No, there hadn't been another time.

I took a shaky breath. Just one Inderal—I should have taken just *one* for this last lesson. I could have. Another bottle of orange pills had appeared magically in my violin case, compliments of Diana. I'd stared at it several times, but hadn't flushed the pills yet. Not that flushing them would do anything. She probably had a stockpile of refills in her medicine cabinet.

"So you are all grown up, no?"

I shrugged, wary of admitting to anything that could be used against me. "I guess so."

"A few months more and you will be at Juilliard."

"Yes."

"New York will be good. It's time."

Speaking of time, why are we wasting it? I wanted to ask. Juilliard was forever away, but the Guarneri was closing in. The whole concept of school in the fall had receded into something hazy, too distant to worry about.

At the very least, we needed to run through my semifinal program today.

"Nothing left," Yuri continued cryptically, talking more to the wall than to me. Then he tapped his finger on his skull and stared at me with bloodshot eyes. Maybe he'd been drinking already this morning. Or maybe those were just the swollen eye sockets a lifetime of vodka had earned him. "Saturday was . . ."

I rubbed the curved wooden arms of the chair and held my breath.

"Saturday was Carmen."

I let the air out and breathed in, the sweet and pungent smell of pipe tobacco filling my head.

"Every competition, every performance, every win, every recording—all perfect because you play like I tell you. Perfect, but not you."

His gnarled fingers uncurled themselves from the pipe stem and rested on the desk. He stared at them. "Your fingers have been good since mine stopped working," he said.

I couldn't not look at his hands. I forced my mind to see them as they might have been when he was young, smoothing out the knobs and wrinkles, straightening the crooks. The image made my heart sore. Would my hands someday be like that?

"These last months have been like this," he said and

brought two fists together, tapping the knuckles against each other like bulls butting heads. "My mistake. You were ready, but I pretended not to see. I thought I could stretch it out, the time for me to play through you. . . ." He had swiveled his chair and stared out the window now. When he continued, it was to himself, more musing, "But I've been lucky. Two careers . . ."

I understood. Even with his vagueness and the accent that I could have sworn was getting thicker the longer he lived in America, he was clear. He was finished with me. It wasn't how I imagined it—he wasn't angry and it wasn't a punishment—but that made it more real. More final, at least. It was a gentler kind of good-bye.

The tears I'd sucked back in front of Clark welled in my eyes again, but this time spilled over and rolled down my cheeks. Yuri didn't notice, or did me the courtesy of not scowling like he would have done any other day.

Regret made everything ache inside of me. Why had I been so impulsive? I'd just tossed off everything he'd been trying to get me to do with the Tchaikovsky without even thinking how he'd respond. I *needed* him. And not even asking him for advice about stopping Inderal, that had been disrespectful and stupid.

My last ounce of hope produced one thought: maybe I could change his mind. But I knew it was hopeless. Begging would repulse him. He was back to puffing on his pipe again, staring into the clouds of smoke as they thickened the air above us.

"This is not sad," he said.

I wiped my wet cheeks on my sleeve self-consciously, and sniffed.

"You don't need me," he continued. "A week ago, how good was Tchaikovsky? Not at all. Now, the way you played on Saturday, you have a chance. You can't win Guarneri playing for me."

I nodded. It was what he wanted me to do.

"And not for Diana."

I looked at my own hands in my lap. My fingers were skinny and strong, their calloused tips peeling at the edges and past the point of feeling.

"I'm sorry," I said.

"No. Be something else."

"Then I'm grateful."

He nodded and then his chin quivered, but so slightly I couldn't be sure it had really happened. He brought his hand to his face and rubbed his eyes irritably. It was just one moment. When he took it away, his face perfectly calm again. "So am I," he said.

Carmen,

Hey. I've been sitting here staring at the

bloody blinking cursor for at least a half
hour. Not sure what to say. Do you hate
me? I give you permission to.

J

I started my reply, deleted the first few words, then
gave the cursor the same half-hour stare Jeremy claimed
he'd given it. I may have been a relationship novice, but
I knew enough to know I shouldn't write what I was feeling (*I'm humiliated because I actually thought you liked me,
angry because you used your dying brother to make me feel like
crap, and oh yeah, I somehow still* do *like you, which means I
have absolutely no self-respect*), but if not what I was feeling,
then what? I looked at the clock. Too late to call Heidi.
I got up and poured myself a bowl of Froot Loops, sat
back down at my computer and stared at the cursor for
another ten minutes.

Jeremy,

I don't hate you. But if I wanted to, I definitely
wouldn't need your permission.

His reply was quick.

Good to see your spunk is still intact.

He wanted banter. I couldn't do banter.

Do you need something?

I paused before I pressed send. It was harsh, but he deserved it.

A second chance.

Unbelievable.

At what? You have to admit our situation makes being friends a little awkward.

He couldn't honestly think we could be together.

So we've got a few complications to work around. So what?

Was he a complete idiot? Had he blocked everything that had happened out of his brain? The other possibility—that I was blowing things out of proportion—wasn't something I was willing to consider.

Jeremy, I wish you the best of luck next
week. I really do.

Did you believe that? Of course not. Me
neither. That's the problem here, or one of the
problems. Neither of us can trust the other's
motives. I think we will both be happier with
ourselves if we let our violins do the talking,
meaning I don't think we should see each
other before the Guarneri. Focus on your
music. I need to focus on mine. May the best
violinist win, and maybe next week after the
finals we can talk. Or whatever.

Pressing send should have felt better. But I was hol-
low. That pang of loneliness in my chest was too heavy to
feel anything more than anger.

His reply didn't make me feel any better.

I'm sorry. I really am. You're obviously mad
and you have every right to be. You're right
about the competition, so I'm not going to
say another word to you about it.

But I do get to tell you that you're wrong.
About my motives, I mean. I didn't do

anything or say anything that I didn't feel.

I promise.

Jeremy

Every part of me wanted to reply. But I couldn't. It wasn't smart, and I had to start being smart if I was going to win.

I *was* going to win, but not for Yuri, and not for Diana. I was going to win for me.

Couldn't exhaustion earn me a good night's sleep? It seemed unfair. But insomnia, or at least *my* insomnia, didn't even give a courtesy nod to what was fair.

That night I crawled into bed so tired my back and shoulders ached, but the music in my head wouldn't stop. There was only one way to quiet it.

I slipped across the hall to where my violin was waiting, the orange wood shining like an exotic flower in the moonlight. I picked it up and played the first few notes of *Claire de Lune*. Moonlight. I walked over to the window while I played and stared up at the same moon. It seemed impossible that Claude Debussy had looked up into the night sky over a hundred years ago in France and heard this melody calling from that same glowing pearl in that same black sea.

Impossible but beautiful, like a fairy tale.

I stopped thinking and just let the notes sing. There was something pure about the melody, free from the tarnish of complications that I seemed so good at inflicting on music by daylight.

The same moon. If it had given Debussy *Claire de Lune*, maybe it would give me something too.

Chapter 15

The Guarneri was upon me.

That final week was a marathon of second-guessing and it all came back to that impossible-to-answer question: What was I most likely to screw up? What would I look back and wish I had spent just a few more minutes practicing? I didn't know: fingered octaves? Just to be safe I had to drill them to death. Or what if I overshot that brutal shift at the end of the cadenza? I'd played it perfectly at least the last dozen times through, but that wouldn't be any consolation if I missed it in performance. And it really could come down to something as painfully simple as that. One missed shift. So I did every shifting exercise I'd ever learned about a thousand times, just in case.

My days were a sad mixture of practicing, eating, and googling illnesses that might put me safely in the hospital and out of the competition. I avoided Diana. Her ice queen act had thawed just enough to reveal paranoia in full flare. I couldn't be around her. Seeing her vacillate between panic and distraction was just a reminder of her doubt, so I spent a lot of time in my room. She didn't intrude. She was too terrified of unsettling my oh-so-delicate sanity to even punish me for lying to her.

Jeremy didn't email or call, but that was good. The humiliation was still there, burning in my chest every time I thought about him, simmering under everything even when I wasn't thinking about him. Fuel. It was fuel, and I had to feed it.

Anger at Diana had helped center me without the Inderal; humiliation over Jeremy might be my only hope at focusing on something outside of my own anxiety. It had to be, which was why I couldn't forgive Jeremy. If I started to wonder if maybe he hadn't been using me, I'd have nothing to anchor myself to when the panic set in. And then I might give in to the urge and take a pill.

I stared at the pile of dresses on my bed. Diana had already chosen one for me, but I was trying on every-thing in my closet anyway. The nos were on the floor, the maybes were on the bed. The dress she'd picked was fine—flowing yellow fabric with a scoop neck and cap sleeves, falling just above the knee—and she'd decided on it weeks ago, back when we'd still been talking. "It's perfect for spring, but not too fancy," she'd said. "It's only the semifinals. You don't want to look like you think you're performing for royalty." She was right. But now I felt like an upside down daffodil in it. I wanted to wear something else. Something I picked.

I pulled the yellow one off the hanger on the back of my door and tossed it on the floor. Then I noticed a sea-green fabric poking out of the stack. I grabbed it and pulled it out. How had I forgotten about this dress? It had a satin sheen, a deep V in the center, and flared out at its floor-length hem. It was probably too fancy.

"Carmen?" Diana's timid three-tap knock sounded on the door behind me.

"What?" I kept my voice was perfectly even—not angry, not penitent, not anything.

She stayed in the hall. "We need to talk about tomorrow," she said. "About your medication."

"No, we don't."

She paused. I'd confused her. "So you'll take it?"

"No."

She exhaled and shivered. "Car—"

"Please leave," I interrupted.

Pleading filled her eyes. "What has happened to you?"

I didn't answer. I wasn't sure, but it *had* happened, and it wasn't unhappening.

"Don't do this," she tried again.

"Good night," I said, and closed the door.

The auditorium was nearly empty. Twenty-five, maybe thirty people sat in clusters scattered across the main floor. From my view through the stage right curtains, I recognized most of them—other competitors who had already played, their teachers, a few parents or friends. The stage was bare except for a single grand piano.

I knew it was impossible, that the judges were too far away, but I swore I could hear the scribble of their pencils, slashing their critiques through the last violinist's performance. Almost my time. I couldn't see Jeremy, but I wasn't expecting him to be there. I pulled back from the break in the red velvet panels and closed my eyes.

In through the nose, out through the mouth, in through the nose, out through mouth.

In one of those middle-of-the-night internet searches that only make sense at the time, I'd looked up Lamaze breathing techniques. My thinking had been: childbirth, performing—they probably weren't that different. Both were high stakes and hugely painful. Both went smoother with drugs, or so I'd heard. Dr. Wright, the Inderal shrink, had given me some relaxation exercises, but I didn't trust anything that came from him.

In through the nose, out through the mouth, in through the nose, out through mouth.

Again, it made more sense in the middle of the night. But I hadn't thrown up yet, so maybe it was working.

I adjusted the bodice of my dress, tucking a wandering bra strap back under the satin. Diana usually loved playing supervisor to those details. Errant strands of hair, smudged eyeliner, loose threads—she usually had them tamed, corrected, or snipped before I even noticed them.

I glanced over at her. She was staring through the part in the curtains, right at the judges' table. She hadn't said anything about the dress change. When I'd come downstairs wearing the sea green gown she'd blinked and turned away, as if she'd never cared in the first place.

I turned back to the audience. The stage lights were only partially dimmed, which meant I could see my competitors' faces. They revealed a little of everything: nervousness, relief, hostility, hope. I checked again to see if Jeremy had slipped in the back, but of course he hadn't. He wasn't playing until tomorrow.

The judges' table sat wedged between the main block of seating and the exit doors, all three judges tucked into it. I squinted, trying to make out their expressions and found myself drawn to just one.

On the far left sat Dr. Nanette Laroche, a cold-eyed French woman in her seventies. For decades she had been *the* teacher to study under at Juilliard. Now retired, she had been a career-maker, and according to legend, her methods made Yuri's look gentle. Dozens of violinists had been squeezed and twisted into world-famous musicians by Dr. Laroche, but her appearance—frail frame, soft features, graying hair—was grandmotherly in every way. Except for those chilly eyes.

The other two judges were less interesting to me. There was Dr. Daniel Schmidt, musical director of the Zurich Symphony, and Dr. Yuan Chang, a professor of music theory at the Curtis Institute. Both seemed too far removed from actual violin performance to be holding all this power.

Beside the main judging table, the competition proctor sat at a little table of her own. It was her job to see that things ran smoothly, which meant ringing the bell for the next competitor, stopping performers if they went over their allotted time, and shushing anyone who got too loud. Tweed jacket, horn-rimmed glasses, excellent posture, face-lifting bun—she looked like she was auditioning for the part of a librarian. Any second now she would ring the bell and it would be my turn.

I took inventory of myself. I hadn't taken Inderal in over a week, but the feelings churning through me were just as bad as that first performance without it.

I felt nauseous, and my hands couldn't get colder, not even if I'd plunged them into a bucket of ice and held them there. My legs were shaky, but I could walk.

I gave the audience one last glance, and this time I saw Clark and Yuri in the far left corner. I'd been too busy looking for Jeremy and missed them before. Yuri sat slumped in his chair, his head nestled into the mountain of his hunchback, his hands folded patiently in his lap. His presence was calming. After my last lesson, I wasn't sure he would come at all. Everything had felt so final when I'd left.

Win it for myself. That was what he'd told me. I was trying.

I'd spent the last week unraveling. Layer after layer peeled off, was still peeling off, and underneath . . . I didn't really know what was underneath.

The metallic ding of the proctor's bell jerked me out of my thoughts. It was time. I took a deep breath and stepped onto the stage. One foot at a time, slowly, evenly, I made my way to the center, barely aware of my accompanist behind me.

I'm okay. Awful but okay. The realization hit just in time. My knees were shaky, but not buckling. My hands were still cold, but I could move them.

The proctor announced me, articulating each syllable. "Car-men Bi-an-chi."

I glanced at the judges' table, put my violin on my shoulder and began to play. Tentative at first, the music began to flow, and then rush, and then soar. I was free, and everything else melted away. And as I lifted my bow from the strings after the final note, I knew it was enough.

Silence, then a thin ripple of applause sounded across auditorium.

"Thank you," said the proctor.

Out of breath, I took one last look at the judges' table. All three were busy writing, heads down, hands scribbling furiously. Weren't any of them going to look at me? As if reading my mind, Dr. Laroche lifted her silver head and nodded.

Ding. The bell was my cue to exit the stage, but I didn't want to pull away from those cold gray eyes.

Ding. "Thank you," the proctor repeated, this time louder with a hint of annoyance.

I nodded back and left the stage.

That night I checked my email over and over, but it stayed empty. When something did come in at 10:37 it was an ad for a male enhancement product, then an H&M sale notice popped up ten minutes later.

Nothing from Jeremy, probably because I'd told him

to leave me alone, and because he was practicing for his semifinal tomorrow. I was dying to send him an email and tell him how well I'd played. He deserved to know. He deserved to be scared.

Finally, I turned off my computer and stretched out across my bed. I missed him. That didn't make any sense, considering how mad I was at him and how hurt I still felt. But that didn't make me miss him less.

I pulled up onto my elbows and grabbed the dog-eared competition schedule off my nightstand. Jeremy played at five p.m. Only one person followed him, then the judges took an hour to deliberate before they announced the three finalists at seven o'clock sharp. Part of me wanted to go early and hear Jeremy play again, but the rational side nixed that idea. I needed to do exactly what I'd told him to do: focus on my own music. I'd show up just before seven.

My head suddenly felt heavy, too heavy to hold up. My performance had been . . . perfect? No. Nothing was ever perfect. But it had been close, nerves and all. I smiled and stretched my arms over my head. The memory of it made everything else unimportant. Or at least less important. I let go of the schedule, letting it fall to the floor and slide under my bed. My head dropped to my pillow and my thoughts glided halfway into dreams, through the different pieces of music I'd been practicing, and then strange music I didn't even recognize. The sound of my violin was beautiful, but it echoed in an empty concert hall and finished to no applause at all.

Chapter 16

I ended up sitting alone waiting for the results to be announced. Diana, inexplicably, needed to use the ladies room. "Right now?" I said, not even attempting to hide my disbelief. I was starting to consider other explanations for her weirdness: Was she sick? Was she depressed? Was she losing her mind? "You'll miss the results," I said.

"Don't worry, you played beautifully yesterday. You'll make the finals," she said, and wandered off in the wrong direction, as if she didn't know exactly where the bathrooms in this building were.

But I wasn't worried. As annoyed as I was with her, I just didn't want to sit alone. When they called out the names of the finalists, everybody would clap and I'd have to stand and smile, and people would see I was by myself. I dug my fingers into my arm, mad that I even cared. I looked around the auditorium, half-filled with all the competitors, their teachers and parents and friends gathered around them. Yuri wouldn't come (he hates this side of competitions—no music, all shmoozing) and Clark had a meeting he couldn't change.

The other competitors all seemed to know each other. They were all older, mostly in their twenties, and . . . and what? Unfriendly? Not exactly. Maybe I was the unfriendly one. Or were they afraid of me? That's what Diana would say.

I took my cell phone out of my purse and pretended to be actively engaged in organizing my contacts.

"If I sit beside you, are you going to tell me to bugger off?"

Jeremy's voice startled me. I moved my purse from the chair beside me. "Go ahead."

He sat down. My insides swirled and twisted over themselves. I couldn't help it.

"I should warn you," I said, glancing at the door. "My mom will be back in a minute."

"You don't think she'd like me?" He gave me an ironic grin. "You'd be surprised. I do pretty well with mothers."

"I'm sure you do. So how did your semifinal go?"

A smile covered his entire face. "Great. *Really* great." I could see he wanted to say more but held back. A fine line separated postperformance glee and bragging.

"I'm sorry I missed it."

His eyes caught mine and held them. "We waste way too much time apologizing to each other."

I looked away.

"I heard yours was pretty spectacular too," he continued.

"Heard?"

"Yeah, you know . . ." He waved a hand at the people around us. "Backstage buzz."

I nodded, preferring he didn't know how little backstage buzz I was in on.

"My time slot didn't help me much. The judges probably barely remember yesterday."

"You don't have to pretend with me, Carmen," he said, and shrugged disarmingly.

He was right. We both knew we were making the finals.

Suddenly the noise around us was gone, and I realized everyone was looking up at the stage. The proctor stood slightly pigeon-toed with one hand on her hip and the other tapping the microphone, wearing the same tight bun and tweed suit combination as yesterday.

"If I can have everyone's attention," she began. The comment was completely unnecessary. She already had every eye in the room. A few chairs squeaked as people sat down, and then the air tightened with silence. She gave a quick nod then lifted her stack of papers up to her face and began reading a list of instructions, explanations, thank yous, and apologies. She could have been reading our horoscopes for all anyone cared. We all kept listening, leaning just slightly toward her. Beside me, Jeremy's leg bounced up and down, the energy practically jiggling out of him. I resisted the urge to put my hand on his knee to hold it in place.

"We'd like to remind competitors that complimentary tickets to the Final Gala Concert on Friday can be retrieved at the . . ."

Jeremy leaned over and whispered in my ear, "My family's flying in tomorrow afternoon. Do you want to go out to dinner with us?"

His breath tickled my neck. And the words, once I could actually think about them, made no sense. I'd just suggested that he wouldn't want to be within ten feet of my mother, and now he was inviting me to meet his family. But besides that, tomorrow night was the night before the finals. I certainly wouldn't be out for a night on the town, and I'd have thought Jeremy would want to be home, or in his hotel room, practicing and sleeping too.

Unless his performance prep had more to do with derailing me than getting a good night's sleep. I clenched my teeth and stared straight ahead. Did he think I was the most gullible idiot in the whole world? Did he think that because I'd let him sit beside me I'd forgotten he begged me to lose the competition on purpose?

The proctor rattled off a list of contributors to the Guarneri Foundation, while I imagined what Jeremy had planned. One last attempt to guilt me, or sway me, seduce me, or bully me, that's what he wanted. I shouldn't have let him sit down.

The bitterness in my voice was impossible to disguise. "I don't think so."

"Not everything I do is part of some evil master plan to destroy you, Carmen. Have you even considered the possibility that I'm not a bad person?"

I'd seen through him. That's why he was annoyed.

Across the hall, the door swung open and Diana's slender form entered. Our eyes met, then she noticed Jeremy and scowled.

"And finally on to the announcement you have all been waiting for." The proctor's voice was suddenly louder, and everyone's focus went back to the stage. "Our three finalists for the 2012 Guarneri Competition in random order." She shuffled her pages, pulling a green cue card to the top. "Luc Portier."

A little shout of triumph burst from Luc's father, who then attacked his son with a bear hug. Once free, a grinning Luc stood and turned around to acknowledge the applause. There was backslapping from those around him and a stifled sob from his mother, while everyone else did their best to clap politely and look happy for him.

The proctor cleared her throat. "Alex Wu."

My heart stopped.

Jeremy's leg stopped bouncing. "What . . ." he whispered, but couldn't find the words to finish. There were only three positions, and the first two belonged to Luc and Alex.

This was not supposed to happen. This had not even been a possibility. Everyone knew the competition was between me and Jeremy. Then shock became fear.

I wasn't going to make the finals.

The fuss around Alex continued, but gradually, I felt all the eyes in the hall pulling away from him and onto me. No, not just me. Us. I looked around. Stare after stare met my gaze. People leaned toward each other and whispered, not even bothering to look away when I stared back. Who could blame them? We were the ultimate spectacle: Jeremy King and Carmen Bianchi, sitting together but apart, waiting for one career to end and the other to take off. I would have stared at us too.

Please God, let me have the last spot. I'll start going to church and I'll stop hating my mother and I'll never ask for anything again.

The proctor cleared her throat, then said, "Carmen Bianchi."

I tried to breathe, but there was no air. *Thank you, thank you, thank you, thank you!* I wanted to jump out of my chair, but my legs were too shaky to lift my body.

"Stand up," Jeremy whispered.

Jeremy. I turned to him. A good-natured smile held up his face, a perfectly composed grin beneath lifeless eyes.

"Stand up, Carmen," he repeated, pressing gently on my shoulder blade, pushing me from my daze. I stood just as the rush of applause crested around me. They were all clapping. Jeremy was clapping. It was loud and percussive, more like a firing squad than applause, but I didn't care.

I was going to the finals.

Instantly, Diana was by my side, hugging, kissing, crying, and Jeremy faded away into the horde.

Chapter 17

Live performances can't be rewound. Listening to a concerto isn't like reading a book where you can flip back to check on some detail, or pause the flow of music just to think. Live music has to be ingested linearly, in one sitting, understood on the musician's terms, in the time and progression the composer ordered. Daydreaming? Miss something? Too bad.

"Focus! Focus! Focus!" Yuri said it all the time, whenever he sensed my mind might be wandering. Somehow, saying it in triplicate was supposed to make it magically easier to do.

I needed life to be less like a concerto and more like

a book. I needed to flip back several pages, maybe several chapters, and find out how things had happened. Clues had been missed. I'd been sleeping, and now everything was racing by too quickly.

We drove home in silence. I stared out the window. Diana just drove.

I had every right to be elated. I was elated. But there was something else too, something I couldn't ignore. Guilt maybe, except that wasn't it. I didn't feel bad about playing my best. I felt bad for Jeremy, that plastic smile holding his face together, but that wasn't it either.

Something wasn't right.

"Congratulations, honey."

I looked up. We were home. Diana turned the key and pulled it free from the ignition. "You're almost there. Friday night is all yours—neither of those guys can hold a candle to you." She couldn't stop smiling. She looked happy for the first time in weeks.

I nodded and smiled too because she was right, and because seeing the real Diana again was a relief. I'd missed her. But I couldn't ignore what had happened either. "I don't understand how Jeremy didn't make the finals. It doesn't make sense."

She sighed. "Just enjoy the good luck."

"But he's *phenomenal*. I know. I heard him play."

"But Carmen, you didn't hear him play today! He must

not have played his best, and that's what the Guarneri is about—not how well you played last week, but how well you play in the competition."

"I guess."

"Let's not ruin the night by arguing about Jeremy King. That's over." She gathered her purse and pulled her cell phone out of the pocket. "Let's try Clark again. He's going to be so proud of you."

We walked into the house, and I took off my heels and hung up my coat while Diana left another message for Clark.

"I'm so tired," I said, more to myself than to Diana.

She flopped down on the couch, tossing her purse beside her. "Me too. What an exhausting day."

"I'm going to bed," I said.

"That's a good idea. I think I'll do that in a few minutes too." She got up and started to pour herself a drink.

"Good night, Mom."

"Good night, honey."

I had just climbed into bed when I heard her phone ring. It was probably Clark, still stuck at the office. I was too tired to talk. I'd talk to him tomorrow.

I closed my eyes and tried to sleep, but something pulled at my memory. It was the sound of Diana's ringtone. At night. That phone call I'd overheard—how long ago had it been? It felt like months, but it wasn't. It was two weeks ago, the night after I'd first seen Jeremy behind Rhapsody. I couldn't even remember what she'd said, just that it had been so bizarre and secretive. Something about money.

I changed into pajamas and crawled into bed, but as tired as I was, sleep wouldn't come. Something about money. Something about money. *Wiring* money. She'd told someone to wire her money, but what could she need money for? Clark made plenty of money, and my record sales and competition earnings brought in a good chunk of change. As my manager she earned a fair percentage of that, and as my mother she had access to all of it. But maybe she needed a lot of money, and maybe it had to be a secret. . . .

I heard Clark come in around midnight, rustle around in the kitchen for a few minutes, then go to bed. The house was perfectly silent. Everyone was asleep, but the more my mind ticked, the further I was from joining them.

Jeremy didn't make the finals. *Jeremy didn't make the finals.* I kept forgetting and then remembering, and each time the realization came with a shock. It didn't make sense. But that one hot kernel festered and festered in my brain, and gradually, a terrible idea began to form around it, and the bigger the idea got and the more I tried to avoid thinking it, the more I *couldn't* hide from it, because it was too ugly and too big and it was swirling around and around, and when I couldn't stand the vertigo for one more second, my mind started screaming it: *What if Diana had paid the judges?*

Suddenly my body felt empty and cold. Drained. My head ached from exhaustion. I just wanted to sleep, to not have that thought burning behind my eyes. But I couldn't pretend it away.

Jeremy should have made the finals. If Diana had anything to do with his elimination, I had to know. I had to have proof. I whispered the word in the dark. "Proof." It felt like a mallet banging on my chest.

I swung my legs out of bed and let the balls of my feet and my toes rest on the cold floor. Part of me wanted to curl back up and hide under my warm covers, but this had to be done now.

Diana's study was the logical starting point, but it wasn't until I flipped on the light and surveyed the room that I realized I had no idea what I was looking for. The massive mahogany desk and file cabinet held too many files to sift through. I pulled on each of the drawers. Only the smallest was locked.

There was usually a reason things were locked.

But the key was not in any of the other drawers, or behind the computer, or under the keyboard. I slid my hand around the bookshelf ledges. Nothing. I pulled up the edges of the area rug. Nothing again. I sat down in her chair and stared at the silver-framed picture on her desk. It was of me, wearing a white sundress and crouching in a field of baby's breath, holding the Strad under my chin, eyes closed. It was one of the rejects from my last CD cover photo shoot.

This was stupid. And hopeless. I didn't even know what I was looking for. If she'd paid the judges in cash there would be nothing to find, except maybe a bank withdrawal slip, which she would never have kept. But that was ridiculous. A briefcase full of money (I pictured tidy stacks of bills bound together with little paper belts) was straight from the movies. She wasn't the mafia, she wasn't a drug dealer, and she wasn't in a movie, but how did people pay bribes in real life?

I rifled through the accessible drawers. The only thing worth noting was the checkbook she used for my violin expenses. I flipped through each duplicate check. $240.42 to Mei-Ling Yee for gown alterations, $235.90 to Wolfgang's String Instruments for a rehair and spare strings, $214.67 to Physical Therapy Associates for massage sessions. This was idiotic—did I really expect to find a copy of a check written out to a judge? I put the checkbook back where I found it.

The phone call played again in my mind. Someone was going to wire her money. That was all electronic, but

I didn't have her banking passwords. She let me use her credit card sometimes, but there'd never been a reason for me to know any passwords.

This was pointless because Diana was too smart. *If* she'd done it, she'd have done it so nobody—not the Guarneri officials, not the police, and definitely not some clueless teenager whose only investigative skills had been gleaned from Nancy Drew—would ever be able to trace it back to her.

Her laptop sat closed on the desk in front of me. I opened it, pressed a button, and waited for the screen to flicker to life.

Without warning, the floor above me groaned. My breath stopped, my heart stopped, my eyes closed, and I listened. Were those footsteps?

I hit the power button on the computer and was out of the chair and to the light switch in less than a second. I flipped it off and stood trembling in the dark room, my head leaning against the towering bookshelf, listening to the blood pound in my ears.

Why was I so scared? She was my *mother*. If I really wanted to know, I should be able to march into her room and ask her. I felt my body reel under the wave of adrenaline and the odd sensation of my blood actually running cold. My brain screamed *Inderal!* before I could tell it to shut up.

Footsteps creaked slowly above my head, making their way across the master bedroom floor, then silence, and the sound of peeing. The toilet flushed, the pipes whirled, and the footsteps shuffled back over my head. I waited—two minutes, five minutes, fifteen minutes, I had no idea how long, but it felt like an hour—until my heart rate returned to normal. Then I sat down in front of the computer again.

I should have wanted to confront her, but it wasn't quite that simple. She was too smart. She'd lie and I might believe her, or worse, she'd admit to it and convince me it was the right thing, or at least the only thing, to do. I wasn't ready. Even with everything swirling black, white, and all shades of gray, I had managed to sink my fingers into one thing: I couldn't be part of this. If Diana had bribed a judge, I couldn't play. I couldn't win.

A few minutes of messing around on the computer told me what I already knew. Diana's banking links were all password protected. Halfheartedly, I tried a few combinations of Clark's name and my name. No luck.

As an afterthought, I tried to open her email. The page came up without a password prompt. She hadn't signed out, but why would she, on her own laptop, in her own home? She had a short list of unread emails that had accumulated over last two days, mostly spam, followed by older stuff, receipts for purchases, a few brief letters from Sony Classical execs about meeting and contract details, a handful of letters from friends. I clicked to the second page, which looked to be more of the same.

Then I saw it. One name. It jumped off the screen and burned itself into my brain. Jonathon Glenn. It was dated twelve days ago. I hadn't seen my dad in four years, hadn't talked to him on the phone in eighteen months.

I opened it and began reading.

Di,

It's taken care of. Don't worry, no paper trail.
And you thought I was good for nothing . . .

Jonathon

Of course. Of course, of course, of course. The money came from my father.

I reread the email. Was there any chance I was misunderstanding? No. What else has a paper trail? Nothing. Just money. And probably a lot of it. A large deposit and withdrawal into Diana's account might look strange if someone was checking for something, but of course he would know how to do it so it never even went through her. A large amount of money taken out of a businessman's account, and probably routed through several Swiss banks first—again, only in the movies? who knew?—that wouldn't be suspicious at all. There would be no proof. Or no more than what I was looking at.

I'd found what I'd wanted, but I didn't feel relieved. My head ached, my throat felt dry.

But how much? That depended on what winning was worth, which was impossible to calculate. A win would make me valuable for life. Every figure I imagined seemed too high and too low.

"One million dollars."

I jumped, banging my knee into the edge of the desk, nearly slipping out of the chair. Diana stood beside the open door, leaning against the frame with her arms crossed over her chest, her charcoal silk robe draped over her thin body. Without her makeup she looked colorless and old, a faded version of herself.

"You scared me." My voice sounded weak. Scared.

"One million dollars," she repeated. Her face was expressionless. "That's what you want to know, right? What you're trying to find out? Or is there some other reason you're snooping around in here in the middle of the night?"

The weight of the number crushed me like a massive wave.

One million dollars. "Why?" I asked.

She looked at me with tired eyes. "Really? You don't know why?"

I did know. She wanted me to win and she thought I would lose otherwise.

"I wish you hadn't figured it out," she said, taking a step toward me with one arm outstretched. "You didn't need to know."

Was I supposed to go to her? Let her hug me and lead me back to bed and forget everything, because I didn't need to know? I rubbed my bare arms with my palms, suddenly cold. I needed to think clearly, but I felt my body pulling in, shutting down.

"Trust me, sweetheart. It had to be done, but you don't need to worry about any of it. Your job is to make beautiful music and you did that yesterday. You'll do it again tomorrow."

"But if I'd *really* done my job well enough," I said, my voice trembling, "you wouldn't have thought you had to."

She shook her head. "Jeremy King's talent isn't something you could have fixed."

"Maybe it wasn't something to be fixed."

Her eyes turned hard and her lip curled into an ugly sneer. "Don't. You. Dare!" She was shaking, and she lifted her hand like she was going to slap me. But she didn't. She let it drop back to her side.

"Do you have any idea of the sacrifices I've made for you?" she spat. "Do you ever stop and think about that, or is it always me, me, me? My entire life has been about *your* career. And for the Guarneri I had to go groveling to your father, sneaking around to the judges, begging and humiliating myself. You don't get to be all high and mighty about what's *right*. Just because you're lucky enough to live on this adolescent plane where everything's so easily classified as right and wrong doesn't mean you get to judge me. I make your life possible. Don't you dare turn on me." She shook her head and rubbed her eyes, then muttered again to herself, "You didn't need to know."

"I didn't *need* to know?" I yelled, surprised at the volume of my own voice, but too furious to lower it. "Are you kidding? I didn't need to know that I am a complete fraud?"

"Stop! It's time for you to grow up. You wanted to win because you were the best, and that would have been wonderful, Carmen, but that was *not going to happen*. Before you lose yourself in a tantrum, stop and think about what I've just done for you. I saved your career, your life, everything we've worked for."

It was true. *We* had worked for it. It had always been *we*.

"But I deserved the chance to . . ." The words fell lamely between us. Chance to what? Lose?

"Deserved? That's a childish way of looking at life. We deserve lots of things. Life is not about getting what you deserve. You have to fight for what you need. I'm doing that for you."

"Not for me," I said. Finally I understood. "For you. You're fighting for yourself."

She shook her head bitterly. "I never got that option. When my career ended . . ." Her voice broke and lifted her fingers to the scar on her throat. "You don't want to know what it feels like to lose music. I won't let that happen to you."

She was talking in circles, about her career, about my career, or both, as if they were connected by a twenty-year-long string that was dragging me along. Or maybe I was dragging her.

But she had something wrong. "I could have won it on my own," I said. It was true. I knew it. Jeremy had sensed it too.

She shook her head, but kept her lips pursed in a thin, tight line. Her eyes answered. *No, Carmen. You couldn't have.*

"You don't know!" I was shouting again, but I was done trying to control myself. "I really could have. Everything is different without Inderal. I'm playing for myself now. I could have—"

"I've been in the audience," she interrupted. "I know things are different, but it isn't *all* for the better. It's more exciting, more passionate, but this is the Guarneri, Carmen. It has to be more than that. It has to be perfect, and it has been far from perfect. You do need Inderal, you just don't realize it because you're on such an emotional high when you're out there, you aren't hearing the little mistakes."

Tears spilled over onto my cheeks before I had time to stop them. Was she right? I didn't know anymore.

"You need Inderal," she continued in a softer voice, "but even with it, you couldn't have beaten Jeremy King. His virtuosity . . ." Her voiced trailed off, and she reached out to cup my cheek with her hand. It was warm and steady. I reached up to hold onto it with both of mine.

"But now I have no choice," I whispered.

She gave me a confused look. "With Inderal? When did you ever have a choice? I know you've had this illusion of it lately, of taking control of your own life, or whatever, but now isn't the time for teenage rebellion. I put up with it because I knew you'd come around. I knew I'd be able to make you see what was best."

"I'm not talking about Inderal," I said. "I have no choice about playing. About winning."

"That doesn't make any sense. Why would you choose not to play? And why would you want to lose?"

"Because it's tainted." I shuddered picturing Jeremy's smile as he tried to convince me to stand for my applause. My hands still clung to Diana's arm, her fingers were still splayed over my cheek.

"I didn't buy a win," she said. "I bought an elimination. You still have to earn your win, Carmen."

"Who took the bribe?"

"Half a million to Chang, and half a million to Schmidt."

"What about Laroche?" I asked. The image of her steel gray eyes and solemn face burned in my mind.

She shrugged and dropped her hand from my face. "We didn't go there. Schmidt and Chang were more than willing when we started talking numbers. The high and mighty Laroche wouldn't have accepted it, anyway. At a certain age, money doesn't mean much anymore."

It was all so sleazy. I felt sick. "What if they'd refused?" I asked. Suddenly I saw the risks she'd taken, saw everything she'd put at stake. "What if they'd turned you in, or what if you—we—got caught?"

"I know what I'm doing," she said calmly, smoothing my hair. "This is how things are done in the real world. Trust me."

"But I don't want it this way."

"You're shocked. You're tired. Let's talk about it in the morning."

"I could tell someone," I whispered, summoning every bit of courage I had. "I could turn you in."

Silence. "Don't be ridiculous. Take a moment and imagine what would happen to your career."

She glared at me, waiting for a response, knowing I didn't have one.

"I'll tell you. You'd be nothing. They love you now, but you'd be amazed how fast people will turn on you. The media would crucify you, Sony would drop you, no orchestra in the world would book you, and they'd be crazy if they did because there would be a grand scale boycott of ticket sales. It wouldn't matter if you were the best violinist in the world. Nobody would hear you play, and then they'd forget you."

Tears welled again, blurring her image. "Why did you do this to me? I didn't want this."

"Carmen, you don't know what you want! I didn't do it *to* you, I did it *for* you!"

"Why?"

"Because I love you!"

I closed my eyes and the tears rolled down my cheeks.

"One million dollars," she said. "That's what I paid for you to be able to shine on Friday. Don't you dare think of wasting it."

I was too tired to fight anymore. She was right about my career. Nobody would touch me if I exposed her. In the eyes of the entire industry, I'd be just as guilty. And as far as fairness was concerned, maybe Jeremy was right. There was no such thing as fair.

I let Diana lead me up to bed, her hand on my back. I

was too pathetic to protest. She pulled the comforter over me and tucked me in, brushing my hair off my cheek with her hand and kissing me on the forehead like I was a little girl. I let her. Surrender was my only option.

I lay in bed and listened to the rain fall. It rained all night.

Chapter 18

On Thursday I ran. Not away, not exactly. I waited for sunrise and the sound of rain to stop, then I got dressed—running shorts, a long-sleeve T-shirt, running shoes—and slipped out.

Chicago woke up scrubbed clean from the rain, skyscrapers gleaming like columns of water. The cold stung my legs as I started to run, but after a minute my skin numbed and I could feel the blood pumping all the way to my toes, pulsing in my ears, warming my fingers. I hadn't run in a while. At ten minutes my lungs ached from the bite in the air. It felt good. Just the right blend of pain and exertion meant I didn't have to think.

Except then everything I was running from caught up with me and my lungs felt like they were going to seize up. I could run, but everything still followed me.

When I got home, Diana was still asleep. I limped upstairs and stripped out of my running clothes.

Diana was right. I couldn't be a nobody, not after everything I'd sacrificed. It wasn't fair. And nobody was exactly who I'd be if I refused to play tomorrow, or if I turned her in. Turned *us* in.

"Suck in."

I obeyed. Diana zipped up the back and arranged the top layer of indigo chiffon so it fell just right. I looked out the window into the dark street.

"Perfect," she whispered.

I turned back to the mirror. The dress was a fairy tale in blue, the layers of the skirt flowing like water from the fitted bodice.

"Tomorrow is your night, Carmen."

I nodded.

"We'll have your hair done up like this with the pearls in it." She took two handfuls of curls and twisted them up onto the top of my head. "You'll look like a princess."

She smiled. She was so good at that, putting on the right face and making herself feel that way. She really believed everything was perfect right now.

"Now go take this off, and get ready for bed. You have to get a good night's sleep tonight."

That wouldn't be difficult. I had barely slept last night, and the weight of today, of *both* days, was more than enough. I'd sleep. I was too exhausted to even check my email.

I didn't get Jeremy's email until Friday afternoon. By then it was too late.

Carmen,

Congratulations. I mean it, but I know you probably won't believe me. I really do, though. I won't lie and say I'm happy for you, because I'm not really happy about anything right now. But no matter how I feel about not playing tomorrow night, I know you deserve to be there. I hope you win. I just can't go listen. I think you probably understand. My family cancelled their flights here, and I'm flying home Saturday morning. It's not how I expected to be going home, but it'll be a relief anyway.

I feel like an idiot for what happened, for asking you to let me win. I should never have done that. I've spent the last few years trying to give my brother some great grand gesture, but I think deep down I know it's never going to be enough. For me, I mean, not him. He's the kind of little brother that thinks I'm a hero even when I'm a complete jerk. I guess what I'm trying to say is that you shouldn't feel bad for me. My winning the Guarneri wouldn't have changed anything for Robbie—it wouldn't have cured him or made things fair. Competition isn't about who needs to win the most. I know that, but I just somehow forgot.

I told you this before, and I know you didn't believe me then, but maybe you'll believe me now. I was never pretending with you. Maybe it would have been easier if I was, maybe I wouldn't feel like such rubbish now if it had all been a game, but it wasn't. You just surprised me. A beautiful, talented girl, showing up every time I turned around—I did what any normal guy would do and fell in love with you. Maybe that's why I feel so terrible right now. Honestly, I don't know where the Guarneri pain ends and the Carmen pain starts.

This is longer than I thought it was going to
be, but it feels good to talk to you, even if I'm
not really talking to you. I miss you. Play your
best tomorrow.

Jeremy

I shuddered. It was too late. The time to make decisions, to be brave and do the right thing, had already come and gone. Or at least that was what I told myself.

I'd already had my hair styled: blown straight, re-curled, then twisted up onto my head with the little pearls embedded exactly as Diana had dictated. My dress was hanging on the back of my door, waiting to be put on, while I sat at my computer in my pantyhose and slip, trying to distract myself until it was time to go.

I'd already taken two Inderal. Diana had brought them in with a glass of grapefruit juice while I was practicing. She'd watched me take them. "Two now to calm you down, and three before the performance," she'd said. "We can talk about weaning you off them gradually after tonight." I didn't believe that, but I didn't argue either.

The numbing was too sweet. I closed my eyes and felt the calm spread through my body like cool water. I had to make it through the night, perform and collect my prize without thinking too hard. I had no choice.

We had to leave in an hour. It *was* too late, but if that was true, why couldn't I stop reading his email, again and again and again, like it could somehow save me from myself? Why couldn't I press delete?

I unclipped my dress from the hanger on the back of my door, and put it on. Diana was right about it. It was perfect. Too perfect for how I felt.

A knock at my door startled me. It was Clark's bang-bang, not Diana's tap-tap-tap. "Are you decent?" he called.

"Yeah." I opened the door.

"Wow," he said, and just stood there. "All grown up."

"Don't get sappy on me, Clark. I'm already a wreck."

"You don't look like a wreck. You always seem calm before you play. Your mother on the other hand is downstairs shaking like a leaf. You'd think she was the one going onstage."

I managed a smile for him, but all I could think about was Jeremy's email.

"I'm supposed to tell you the Glenns are coming to the performance tonight, and that they want to take you out for dinner tomorrow—a *celebratory* dinner."

"I'd rather just go for pizza with you."

"Maybe you should tell them that. It's your celebration, right?"

Not really, I thought. *Not at all.* "I guess."

"I just came up to wish you good luck. I'm so proud of you." He paused, looking embarrassed. "You've just turned out to be such an amazing young woman."

Now was the time to tell him. To say it and end this whole horrific thing.

I looked away. If he saw into my eyes he'd know—everyone would know how far from amazing I was.

He stepped forward to hug me and I melted into his warm arms. "Your best is always good enough for me, Carmen," he whispered into my ear. "You know that?"

I nodded, and willed the tears not to come.

"Just do your best."

His words felt like a kick in the stomach. My air was gone.

He released me and turned around to go. "Your mom says we're leaving in forty-five minutes," he called over his shoulder. "I'll go make you some dinner. Salmon and quinoa: brain food and slow-release energy. You'll be unstoppable."

I couldn't answer. Still no air.

My best. This was not my best. Jeremy and Clark, they loved a Carmen that didn't even exist anymore. But if she didn't exist, if I'd traded her for music, maybe music wasn't worth having.

* * *

Slipping out wasn't hard.

I could hear Diana in her room putting her makeup on, getting ready to go, and Clark in the kitchen, banging around with a pot and a spatula while shouting at the ref for whatever sporting event he was watching.

First, I packed up my laptop and slid it into the top of my violin case. Then I put my heels on, slung my violin over my back, and flipped off the light switch. As an afterthought, I went back to my desk and scribbled a note:

I went to fix things.
—Carmen

I left the note on my bed, then I tiptoed down the stairs and out the front door. Catching a cab was easy; deciding where to go was not. "Can you just drive around for a few minutes?" I asked the cab driver.

He looked like a chain smoking Santa, from bushy beard to round pink cheeks. "Sure," he said, and shrugged as if teenage girls in evening gowns were always asking him to circle the block on Friday afternoons. He flicked a cigarette butt out of his window. "Got a machine gun in there?" he asked pointing to my violin case, and chuckled.

Hilarious. I smiled politely. "Sure do," I said, then stared out the window so he'd stop talking to me and let me think. A breeze ruffled the leaves on the poplars that lined the street. I wanted to be outside, away from people, but not alone. Maybe the beach.

"Can you take me to Michigan Avenue and Lakeshore?"

"Sure, " the cab driver said. "Just past the Drake?"

"Yes, please."

The cab sped up, and I tried to distract myself by peering into the windows of the cars we passed. Backseat people-watching was usually good entertainment, but my mind refused to be diverted. I couldn't stop trying to picture what Jeremy would do when he found out. Kick a hole in the wall, maybe. Swear. Cry. I felt like I knew him so well, but I didn't. I'd never even seen him angry. And I didn't know if he'd hate me forever, or if some day he'd look back and see it wasn't my fault.

Clark's reaction would be something else. He wouldn't hate me, but he would be furious with Diana. And that would be my fault. They'd been married for ten years, but betrayal was something people got divorced over. I forced my mind forward. I couldn't think about the possibility of losing Clark if I was going to go through with this.

"Here we are," the driver said, pulling over to the curb.

I paid him, and pulled myself—gown, violin, computer, and all—out of the cab.

In front of me the beach stretched left and right, icy lake edged with toast-colored sand. From the looks of the thinning crowd, it had been just warm enough for the brave ones to swim, but the air was already cooling and most people were out of the water. Clusters of shivering, sandy people, wrapped in towels and huddled around picnic baskets dotted the beach.

I took off my shoes and hooked the heels around my violin case strap. The sand felt dry and crunchy beneath my feet as I walked halfway to the water's edge. I chose a spot just far enough away from people to avoid getting stupid comments about my beach attire, then I put down my violin case and sat on it.

My computer was slow to boot up, so I surveyed the beach while I waited. The sun, floating just above the waterline, glowed a burnt shade of orange. It was the same color as my violin. I looked away, my eyes aching from the glare, and positioned myself sideways so I could see my screen without the sky behind it. I was running out of time.

I opened my email, clicked on "New" and began to type, feeling the sun sink beside me as I wrote. By the time I was done, the lower lip of the sun was just barely melting into the horizon, spilling fire into the lake. I read the email over. Not perfect. But good enough.

I had just enough time to find the email addresses I needed. Most of them were in my contacts list, and the others weren't hard to find. The trickiest were the competition organizers and the three judges, but the Guarneri Competition had a decent website.

I read it over one last time. If I was going to send it, it had to be now. The concert was supposed to start in a half hour. I looked over to the blazing horizon. The lake had become a pool of lava under the half-dipped sun. I took a deep breath and tapped send.

I'm writing to explain why I won't be performing tonight. Hopefully at least one of you gets this email in time. I'm sorry I didn't write it sooner, but once you all read what I've written, I'm sure you'll agree with my decision to withdraw.

On Wednesday evening, several hours after the announcement of the three finalists, I discovered that Dr. Daniel Schmidt and Dr. Yuan Chang each received $500,000 to exclude Jeremy King from the finals. I can't explain how I found out or who paid them. I know I look guilty, but it wasn't me, and if I had done it I wouldn't be writing this email. I just had to come forward. It has also occurred to me that the two judges in question could simply deny the accusation,

and I certainly don't know anything about
tracking money or looking into bank records
or any of that. I'm guessing, though, that
Dr. Laroche would have an opinion as to
whether or not her colleagues were biased.
I find it very unlikely that she agreed with
their decision not to advance Jeremy.

You're all probably wondering why I waited
until now. I wish I had a better reason, but
honestly, I didn't come forward earlier
because I wanted to win this competition.
I've always wanted to win. At least I thought
I did, but now I know what I wanted was to
be the best. Winning tonight wouldn't prove
that. The best is completely irrelevant now.
Again, I'm sorry.

Carmen Bianchi

I sat and watched the sky turn from orange to pink to
violet and then darken. The wind blew and I shivered. If I'd
have been thinking when I left the house, I'd have brought
a sweater instead of my violin. Why had I brought it? Habit.
I never went anywhere without it, but tonight it was just a
useless weight to lug around on my back, a place to park my

butt on the beach. A burden. I never wanted to play it again. Not that it mattered. My career was over anyway.

I thought I'd feel better once the email was sent, but I didn't feel better at all. I didn't feel anything. Probably the Inderal.

A gust of wind picked up sand and whipped it at me. It was time to go, but I had nowhere to go to. I twisted my body and looked up toward the towers at the north end of the Magnificent Mile. The Drake. I wondered if Jeremy was in his room.

Chapter 19

The balcony felt cold under my cheek. Ten floors below me the traffic of Lake Shore Drive purred, but it seemed miles away. Everything before me was perfectly still: a black starless sky over Lake Michigan, my bare arm jutting out between metal bars, and the burnt-orange scroll of my violin rising out of my clenched fist.

It would be as easy as opening my hand. I could just uncurl my fingers one by one, and when the last one relaxed, the violin would slice the night sky like a blade, plummeting to the ground below. Then it would be over.

I exhaled and felt my body flatten against the concrete. My mother would be furious about the gown. Her personal dressmaker had twisted and tucked and pleated the filmy chiffon until it looked like a waterfall, flowing cascades in three shades of blue. Now it was bunched beneath me, probably soaking up dirt, grease, cigarette ash, and whatever else hotel balconies collected.

What was I thinking? The gown was the least of Diana's worries.

Jeremy hadn't been in his room, but it was easy to get in. I'd just had to convince one of the maids I'd locked myself out.

I shivered. The wind swirled around me, picking up black curls and whipping them against my cheek and bare back. The hair clips and bobby pins were long gone—they'd been the first things I'd removed after stepping inside the room. Then I'd kicked off my heels, peeled off my stockings, and pulled out my earrings. Nothing had worked. That had been an hour ago and the tightness was still everywhere, my chest, my head, my calves, my fingers.

So I'd taken my violin out of the case and onto the balcony.

It was hard pinpoint exactly when the idea had come—if I'd known when I'd broken into Jeremy's room, or if I'd imagined it when I'd first walked out onto the balcony with my instrument in my hand. Maybe not even then, maybe not even as I lay flat, dangling the violin over the edge.

$1.2 million. The figure was hard to understand. Hard

to *feel*. I let the violin sway, just a little, and closed my eyes. *Murder*. The word came to my mind and I dismissed it. That was ridiculous. The violin wasn't alive. It wasn't a baby or an animal, not living.

But that would be easier to believe if I hadn't felt it breathe and sing.

I opened my eyes. My knuckles, bony and white, were shaking. The pills were wearing off. The music was over.

I opened my hand, and at the very moment I felt the wood begin to slide I heard Jeremy roar, "No, Carmen!" I looked up to see him hurl his body into the railings just above my head, his arm shooting through the gap between the bars, his fingers wrapping around mine and around the scroll. It took a moment to feel the weight of his body, crushing me, and the pain in my crumpled fingers.

I couldn't breathe. He rolled off me, pulling the violin and my arm back through the railings. With his other hand, he gripped the Strad, then finally released my crumpled fingers. I couldn't sit up, I didn't have the strength, so I stayed on my back staring at the black sky.

"Are you crazy?" he shouted, getting up on his knees and staring down at me.

Was I? My body ached, but my mind was empty. "Maybe," I whispered.

He gasped, still catching his breath and leaned back

on his heels. "I walked in and saw you out here. I thought you were going to . . . you know . . . kill yourself." He glanced over the balcony as if to confirm it was in fact high enough.

I shook my head slowly. "That hadn't even occurred to me."

"Was it your mom?"

I nodded. "You got the email."

"Yeah. I was sitting at Lavazza, drinking my fourth espresso and considering a career in online poker when it popped up."

"Do you hate me?"

He paused. Then he shook his head no.

"This cement is freezing."

"You could sit up," he said.

I didn't have the energy.

"Jeez, Carmen. I can't believe you were about to drop your Strad off the Drake." He shook his head, then pushed his hair out of his face.

A siren approached and retreated far below us.

"What happens now?" I asked.

"I have no idea. We wait, I guess. I'm going home tomorrow."

"But . . ." I didn't know how to finish.

"But what happens to you?"

I sniffed, pulling back tears.

"I don't know, Carmen." He put his hand on my cheek, then in my hair. "You're kind of screwed. You love music?"

I looked at my Strad nestled tightly in the crook of Jeremy's arm.

"Aside from wanting to drop your million-dollar Strad off a balcony, do you love music?" he repeated.

"Yes. Always. But I don't think I can come back from this."

"You mean professionally?"

"No, but that's true too. It's more about not knowing if I want to."

He nodded. He understood.

"You need to get out of here," he said. "Away from this place. Away from her."

"Why don't you hate me? I've ruined everything for you."

He waited a moment, then shook his head. "I just can't. And it wasn't you. You did the right thing, Carmen."

"Where could I go?"

He didn't answer. There was no answer.

Jeremy held me all night.

At first he pulled me onto his lap, and we sat huddled on the balcony, his arms wrapped around me and his chin resting on my head. But then the wind grew sharper and not even his warm arms tight around my rib cage could hold in the shivering, so he picked me up and carried me inside. Despite everything, it felt right. He laid me on his bed, took a blanket from the closet and lay down behind me, pulling our bodies together under the blanket. Maybe it had been the most horrible day of my life, but the heat of his body, his breath on my neck, the pressure of his hand resting on my hip—that was close to perfect.

As long as I didn't think about the carnage (my career, my family, my whole life) I would be all right, but I couldn't keep my brain from poking at it. It was too fresh. Everything was over. And my mother . . . I didn't know if she would ever talk to me again, or if I even wanted her to. I closed my eyes and tried to close my mind. I needed to force the thoughts out and just feel things instead. Like the smell of Jeremy's skin, or the rise and fall of his chest. Those were warm and real and safe, but my mind wouldn't obey. It kept coming back to that one thing.

"Jeremy . . ."

"Yeah?"

"The Guarneri." The word tasted like bile in my mouth. "It should have been yours."

His voice was deep and slow. "Maybe. Or maybe it should have been yours."

I squeezed my eyes shut even tighter and pictured him on stage. "I'm sorry," I whispered again.

He breathed in and out, labored and deliberate. "Me too."

I was an idiot. Lost in my own pain storm, I'd forgotten about what he must be feeling. But even that, the fact that he was hurting too, was something the self-centered soloist in me couldn't quite accept. His loss was temporary. He would win more competitions, maybe even the Guarneri in four years. I wouldn't. I would never perform again.

Never? My heart started beating quicker, that familiar panic returning. *What have I done?* I suddenly gasped for air and clenched my fists, feeling tears flood my eyes.

"What's the matter?" Jeremy asked. "You're practically shaking."

"I don't know," I whimpered, embarrassed, but not able to control it. "I just remembered everything all over again, and I can't believe it really happened." The tears spilled over, trailing sideways streaks across my face and onto the pillow. "What did I do? I burned every bridge in sight and now where am I supposed to go? What am I supposed to do now?"

"Shhh," he said. "Tomorrow. Let's worry about it tomorrow."

"But—"

"Relax, Carmen." He rubbed my arm with his open palm and kissed my bare shoulder. "In the morning we'll start fixing things."

Relax. He made it sound easy. I let go of the breath I was holding and tried releasing my tension, one muscle at a time. My calves, my back, my fists, my jaw, my fingers, everything ached as I slowly unclenched—ached, but sang with relief too. I could almost feel my body melting into his. By the end I was calm enough to feel his heart beating behind mine, anchoring me, and the last thing I remembered before falling asleep was the absolute rightness of Jeremy's lips on my shoulder.

When I woke the first time it was still dark. But even before I was awake, before I thought about opening my eyes, I felt the weight of Jeremy's arm still wrapped around me and his breath on my neck. I wasn't ready for morning to come. Not yet. Once I was awake and he was awake and life started happening again, I couldn't be sure there would ever be another moment like this, so I lay perfectly still, eyes closed, soaking up the sweetness of it. The earliest-rising songbirds had started to chirp, but my mind was stronger. I forced myself back to sleep.

It must have been hours later when I woke again. This time the brightness of the room left me no choice and I opened my eyes. Light gleamed through the windows on both sides of Jeremy's corner suite.

"Jeremy," I whispered, but I already knew he was gone. The bed felt empty around me.

There was a note on his pillow.

Carmen,

I went to your house. Don't be mad. Your stepdad called my phone (I guess you left your phone at home) and told me to come by early while your mom is out. I'm bringing back some stuff for you—clothes and things, just to give you some time to decide what you want to do. I'll be back soon.

Jeremy

Clark called Jeremy? He must have guessed where I was, or figured it out from my phone or maybe my email. But did Clark want Jeremy to get some of my stuff, or was that Jeremy's idea? I reread the note. I couldn't tell. If it was Clark's idea, that meant Diana was mad enough to kill me and he was trying to keep us apart. Or maybe he thought I was mad enough to kill her. Maybe I was.

I stood and twisted the corseted bodice of my dress back into place. The boning had been digging into my ribs all night, and I had to assume I'd have permanent lines up and down my torso if I ever took the dress off. Was it only yesterday that I'd put it on? It felt like a full week had passed since then.

Jeremy's suitcase lay unzipped at the foot of the bed. I flipped open the top and started rifling through the tidy little piles for something to wear. But then I realized what those piles meant, what I'd known but somehow forgotten. Jeremy was packed. Jeremy was flying home today. I closed the suitcase, the room suddenly spinning. Last night he'd said we would start fixing things in the morning. I'd felt safe, or at least not alone. I shouldn't have. He was leaving.

The dizziness worsened and I stepped back from the suitcase. My stomach groaned. Food. I hadn't eaten in . . . I couldn't remember.

I was looking frantically for the minibar key when Jeremy walked in. His face was whiter than chalk, and his eyes shone. He looked crazy. Or was that glee? It seemed like I should be able to tell the difference, but the intensity in his eyes could have gone either way. One of his hands gripped the handle of a familiar leather suitcase, one of Clark's, and the other clutched his phone and a booklet.

I swallowed and waited. I just couldn't ask. But Jeremy didn't say anything, just stood in the middle of the room, staring at me with fire in his eyes.

"So you went to my house?"

He tossed the small navy book in his hand onto the bed. It was a passport. My passport. "I thought I could convince you to come to England with me," he said in a shaky voice.

"I thought we could spend the summer at Gigi's together. But then on my way back here I got a call."

He looked down at his hand. It was still clutching the phone in a white-knuckled grip. Then he looked back up at me. A tight grin had split his face. "It was the president of the Guarneri Foundation offering me an apology. He said he was contacting all the semifinalists. They canceled the finals last night, Carmen."

I waited for more. Of course they canceled it. I knew they would when I wrote the email, and he had to have assumed the same thing when he read it. So why was he freaking out now?

"I guess having two crooked judges and only two finalists left them no choice. They're going to start over."

"What?"

I saw it now. He wasn't angry, he was ecstatic. He shook his head and started to laugh, releasing his death-grip on his cell and tossing it onto the bed beside my passport. Still laughing, he pushed his hair up and out of his eyes, leaving his hand on top of his head.

I reached out and steadied myself on the armoire. Of all the outcomes I'd imagined, I'd never even dreamed of redemption. Actually putting the whole competition together again—it was perfect. But impossible, wasn't it? There were no do-overs in music. If things weren't fair, people sucked it up.

"The whole competition," he continued, dropping the suitcase and pacing the length of the room, "starting with the *same* semifinal list, is being repeated again next week, but with new judges." The smile had taken over his face, stretched his features past their limits. It looked like it hurt. He bounded over the coffee table between us and grabbed me, pulling my body into his. *"Carmen, we get another shot,"* he whispered into my ear.

I closed my eyes. I wanted to feel it. I wanted a piece of his elation, for my heart to be launching itself into orbit alongside his. But it wasn't. I should have been flying, sobbing, throwing my arms around him, feeling *something*. But I was frozen.

Jeremy's grip on me loosened. "What?"

"We don't get another shot," I whispered. *"You* get another shot."

"No, you don't understand, Carmen. They aren't punishing you. They know you didn't do it and they're letting *all* of us play again. I asked that specifically. You're getting another chance too."

I let his words clear the air and enough silence follow for him to hear my every word. "But I don't want it."

Jeremy stopped grinning. "Yes, you do. You're just in shock."

"No." My voice was calm. The dizziness was fading slowly, leaving my mind clear. Everything around me finally stood solid and still. "I really don't." It was true. I knew it now.

"I don't understand," he said, shaking his head. "You aren't thinking this through."

"I am. It's tainted. For me, I mean."

He blinked, still wanting to absorb my sadness into his happiness. "So it doesn't fix anything for you, then," he said.

"No, it does. I'm relieved. I'm choosing this for me."

He put his hand on my cheek, ran his fingers down my jaw and over the violin scar that wasn't a scar at all. "But Carmen, this is the Guarneri. Are you sure?"

Was I? I nodded. I needed time. I needed distance from Diana. I needed to decide why I was playing the violin anyway. Tears welled up in my eyes, and I blinked them back, hoping he didn't see.

"You're sure, but you're not okay," he said.

"No. But I will be."

Chapter 20

My feet hit the sand, right-left, right-left, right-left. Two steps to push the air out of my lungs, then two steps to pull it back in.

Running on sand didn't hurt anymore, but during those first few weeks my lungs had been on fire. Compared to running on pavement, it felt like gravity had been tripled: sinking into the sand then having to pull my feet back up and out. And then afterward, my calves and my hamstrings ached.

But the muscle soreness didn't last long, just a few days. My lungs took longer, around two weeks, to stop screaming in pain and accept that beach running was here to stay.

Mornings like this one were perfect for it. I ran at low tide over the wet sand. It was foggy and still cool, but not so cool that I had to wear more than just my running shorts and sports bra.

No music. Silence was better. As for the sounds I couldn't turn off—the *whoosh* of the surf, the cawing seabirds, the occasional barking dog—those were allowed.

For eight weeks, the music part of my brain had been quiet. Until last night.

I forced my legs to pump faster. This had to be what a gazelle felt like, fast and boundless. Just eight weeks into my marathon training schedule, and I already felt like I could run the entire shoreline of the British Channel.

But not today. Today Jeremy was waiting.

He'd arrived last night on the train from London, looking crumpled and exhausted. His hair was messy, like he'd been sleeping on the train, and probably the plane before that, but his eyes were blue and clear as always.

We hadn't seen each other in six weeks. I'd worried he would be different, or I would be different. What if his win had changed him? We'd only had just that one week together before he'd flown to Singapore, the beginning of his first leg in a year of touring. Watching him leave, that's when I knew I loved him, right when I realized there was nothing tangible tying him to me.

Last night after we'd arrived home from the train station, Gigi had made up a bed on the couch and Jeremy had collapsed into a jet lag–induced coma. Of course, I couldn't sleep. I was dying to tiptoe down from my attic room and just watch him breathe. Instead, I'd lain in bed and heard music in my head for the first time since the night of the Guarneri. I'd finally fallen asleep, but the music had bled into my dreams and was still there when I woke up.

I should have known that seeing him would remind me. I hadn't played the violin since that day. I hadn't played a violin in *eight weeks*. I didn't even own a violin any more. Me. Carmen Bianchi.

I'd left the Strad in Chicago, then dropped a letter in the mail to Thomas and Dorothy Glenn. "Thank you, but I no longer need the violin," was all it said. That was enough. If they wanted more they could talk to Diana.

I smiled. Imagining that conversation always made me smile.

Right-left, right-left, right-left. I loved taking the rhythm of it and speeding up, making my feet push off the beach even faster. Ahead of me the fog was thinning, slowly rolling inland, and I could see where the path to Gigi's cottage split a row of waist-high stones that lined the beach.

And there was Jeremy sitting on a rock, leaning back on his palms.

I slowed to a walk, but my heart refused to stop

pounding. When I was close enough I called, "I thought you'd still be sleeping."

"Me too."

"Aren't you still on Bangkok time?"

"I don't know what time I'm on anymore, but the birds outside my window are no respectors of time zones."

I stopped several feet shy of him. Just seeing him, knowing he was here, that I could touch him and see his eyes when he talked to me, still felt unreal. The blood pounded in my fingertips, at my neck and temples.

"Why are you standing way back there?"

"I'm sweaty."

"I don't mind."

I took the last few steps toward him, and as I did, he leaned forward to put his hands on my waist and pull me the rest of the way. Then he held me there between his knees, his fingers warm on my wet skin.

"A month was too long," he said. "I missed you."

Say it again. "I can't believe you're only staying for two weeks. Your next concert is in Buenos Aires, right? What are you playing?"

He stared over my shoulder at the ocean. "I don't know. What should we do today?"

I tipped my head forward so my forehead rested on his shoulder. "You don't have to do that."

"What?"

"You don't have to change the subject." I lifted my head, put my hand on his cheek, and turned his face so he had to look me in the eye again. "You can't *not* talk about violin."

"Carmen . . . I don't want to hurt you."

I shook my head. "I'm okay. Really."

He half smiled. He didn't believe me.

Was I? I thought so. "It's the truth. Not at first. At first I missed violin so badly my whole body hurt and the only thing I could do was run and run until I wanted to throw up."

"I'm sorry," he said, looking down.

"No, *you* shouldn't be sorry."

"I'm just sorry that all of this happened to you."

"But I'm better now. I miss it, of course, but . . . It's hard to explain."

He kissed my forehead and I shivered.

"Cold? Here, sit." He made room for me and I sat in front of him with his arms around me. In front of us, the sun shimmered, pushing the last wave of fog over us.

Now, Carmen. Do it now.

"I have to tell you something," I said. I took a deep breath. I'd planned out every word, then decided I would never tell him, then changed my mind, and changed it back again. But now the indecision was gone. It was right, not because I had to confess, or because he deserved to know, but because I wanted him to understand.

"Have you heard of Inderal?"

Silence. The pause felt like minutes. Then he said, "Of course. I know a few people who take it. Maybe more than a few."

Facing the ocean, not wanting to see the disappointment on his face, I told him everything. I started with that terrible performance in Tokyo, then Diana and Dr. Wright, needing more and more, and then the night I decided to quit—the night he first kissed me.

Jeremy didn't move. His arms stayed wrapped around me, no looser or tighter than before. But his silence felt heavier than the entire ocean. I went on.

Telling him about quitting was easier. I was starting to feel like that was something to be proud of. I'd stuck it out, and every one of those painful moments belonged to *me*. Not Carmen the violinist, just Carmen.

I finished and waited. He drew a deep breath and held it. What else was he holding in?

"I can't believe you went through that by yourself," he said finally.

By myself? "I had no choice."

"Yes, you did. You could have kept taking it, kept doing what they told you to do. Just like you had a choice when you found out about your mom buying the judges."

Maybe. But I hadn't felt like I was making a choice.

I'd felt defenseless, bullied into a corner I could only crawl out of.

"I'm thinking that, after my brother, you're the strongest person I know."

Relief washed over me. He didn't think I was weak. He didn't hate me either.

"And I'm thinking you must be dying to play," he said. "I know I would be. Do you want me to leave my old violin for you?"

"No," I said. "Maybe."

"Afraid it'll get in the way of your intense running schedule?"

I laughed. "Exactly."

"I feel bad I can't be here for your marathon."

"It's okay. Gigi said she'll hold a sign at the finish line for both of you."

"A sign? She'll probably rent a plane and have it fly a CONGRATULATIONS CARMEN! banner around for the day. She loves you."

"Hmmm." Gigi loving me—that had been an unexpected gift. She'd taken me in and babied me like I was hers. And for no reason. "An airplane banner. I'll take it. Not exactly the kind of fame you're earning yourself this summer . . ."

"I know." He is voice was suddenly serious again. "That worries me."

"Why? What could you possibly have to be worried about?"

"I'm scared violin will always come between us."

I stood up, turned around, and took his hands. "I won't let it."

He didn't respond.

"I won't let it," I said again, pulling him up.

He answered by bending down and whispering in my ear. "Then come with me."

Everything inside me screamed *yes*, but I couldn't say it. I couldn't think.

Then come with me.

Being with him all the time. It was exactly what I wanted, except being on the tour that might have been mine, following Jeremy around while he lived my dream—that would kill me.

I shook my head.

He smiled. He knew. He'd known before he asked.

"Then let's pretend. Have you ever been to Argentina?" he asked.

I could pretend. "Twice. But never as a roadie. Would I get to join your fan club?"

"You'd *have* to join my fan club. I think they're looking for a president."

"Really? Does the president get special privileges? Rosining your bow? Polishing your violin? Would I get to keep your old broken strings to use in my Jeremy King scrapbook?"

"Of course. But you'd just have to promise to behave yourself. No stealing my underwear and selling it on eBay, for example."

"Hmmm. I can't promise I won't do that."

"Then you can't come." He looked me in the eye. "I just wish I didn't have to miss you all the time."

"I'm sure you didn't miss me *all* the time." I just hoped he had.

"No, I did. Last week I was standing in front of the Great Wall of China, and all I could think of was how I'd rather be at a White Sox game next to you pretending I liked baseball."

"*What?* You don't like baseball? Why didn't you tell me?"

"I don't completely *hate* baseball." He took my hand and started walking up the beach toward Gigi's. "Should we go back? Gigi was making strawberry scones when I left."

"Strawberry scones?"

"With clotted cream and strawberry jam."

"Then, yes. We should definitely go back."

When we got back, I went upstairs for a bath. Gigi had no shower—a fact so bizarre I hadn't believed it when Jeremy first told me. Apparently lots of old houses in England didn't. I hadn't been homesick at all so far, but I came close every time I thought about taking a good post-run shower.

Scrubbed clean and dressed for the day, I found Gigi and Jeremy sitting on the back patio overlooking the rose garden.

"How was your run, dear?" Gigi asked, putting her dainty cup back on its saucer and pouring tea into mine. She looked like an aging Hollywood starlet, tall and thin like Jeremy, her silver hair braided and coiled up into a bun. She had all the elegance of Grandma Glenn, but none of the ego.

I loved this part of our morning ritual. Gigi and I had tea every morning when I got back from running. I loved it even more with Jeremy here.

"It was nice." I took a seat and reached for a scone.

"It started out so cold this morning," she said. "I was worried about you."

"I was fine. The fog lifted and it warmed up," I said. "It might even be hot by this afternoon." Another British custom that'd grown on me: discussing the weather.

"A perfect summer day," Jeremy said.

"Let's hope," Gigi said. "You kids can have some fun in the ocean if it gets warm enough."

She poured tea into my cup while I slathered clotted

cream and strawberry jam on my scone. Clark would love these things.

"Oh, I forgot to mention it last night," Gigi said in the same casual tone she'd used for the weather, "but your mother called while you were picking up Jeremy at the train station."

I took a sip of my tea, feeling both sets of eyes on me. This was the fourth time Diana had called. The first time I'd refused to talk to her, then spent the evening in my room so Gigi wouldn't see me seething, fists clenched, screaming into my pillow. I'd refused to talk to Diana the next two times she called too, but then at least I'd been smarter and gone running.

There was no way Gigi'd forgotten about Diana calling last night. She just hadn't wanted to ruin the evening.

"She asked me to have you call her back," Gigi added.

I put the cup back down carefully, but the china still clinked. "Okay."

Gigi raised an eyebrow for just a moment, then let it drop. "You only get one mother."

I didn't look at Jeremy. I couldn't ask him to forgive Diana.

I wasn't even sure if *I* could forgive her. What would I say to her? I was still so mad I had to clench my teeth when I thought about any of it: the bribery, the Inderal, the lifetime of love that depended on my success as a violinist.

But I missed her. Not even the anger could change that, because she was still my mom.

I did the math. It was five hours earlier in Chicago, so she'd be sleeping now. "I'll call her this evening."

"Good," Jeremy said.

Was that sarcasm? Jeremy had no reason to forgive the woman who'd nearly destroyed his career. I looked into his face. His jaw was set with the same determination I'd come to expect, and his eyes were sincere. I wanted to put my hand on his cheek and kiss him. Later. "Really?"

"Really."

The taste of strawberries was still in my mouth as Jeremy and I walked to Charminster to check email. (Gigi refused to get connected with a passion I had to respect, even if it was incredibly inconvenient.) The road to the village was a mile and a half long. I walked it almost every day, but it was so pretty the length didn't bother me, not even after a run. The trees had long delicate branches with leaves that quivered, and wildflowers grew along both sides of the road. Walking it with my fingers laced with Jeremy's, it was even prettier. And when he stopped and kissed me, the lane took on a beauty like I'd never seen.

Gemma's Bakery and Café, my usual Wi-Fi stop, was just busy enough: There was the right amount of bustle to blend into, but we could still hear each other's voices.

Gemma kept her apparently successful business plan advertised next to the baked goods in the window. The sign read, COME FOR THE WI-FI, STAY FOR THE DANISHES.

Gigi was a friend of Gemma's mother, so the owner always welcomed me with a smile and usually a free cup of hot chocolate. Today, when she saw Jeremy, she clobbered him with a hug, then gave us the table by the window with a view of the big stone church across the street.

"That church," I said as I opened up my laptop. "It reminds me of one in downtown Chicago. Do you remember? That beautiful one with the courtyard near the Drake."

Jeremy took a newspaper from a stack behind him and sat across from me. "I know the one you're talking about, but *that* church," he gestured out the window, "is older than America."

I sighed. "Of course it is. Did I really just try to compare British and American architecture? How insensitive of me."

He grinned and folded the paper open to the crossword puzzle.

I looked over my new emails. Spam, spam, spam, delete, delete, delete, but then an address jumped off the screen: nanettelaroche@juilliard.edu. I knew that name. My finger shook as I brought the cursor over the email and clicked. Two months of hard-earned calm drained away.

Dear Miss Bianchi,

I have spent the last two weeks angry.
Finally, this morning, I found myself just
enough *less* angry to be able to sit down
and write this letter to you. For the record,
I detest email. The informality offends me.
I would call you if I had your telephone
number, or stop by and have this
conversation in person if I had any idea
where you were, but I don't. Besides, I fear
what I would do to your mother if I found
her instead. That leaves email.

Your little letter, by the way, created quite
a storm, but I'm sure you know that. If I
had written you directly after your grand
confession—in the midst of the Guarneri
Foundation's humiliation with all those
newspaper articles circulating *world*wide,
and the absolute decimation of credibility
the classical music industry suffered—it
would not have been a pleasant note.
Hate mail, dare I say. However, as I
mentioned before, I am now *less* angry,
and though I'm not known for giving

compliments, I can generally say what
needs to be said, when it needs to be said.
So. Thank you. Your bravery is rare.

It may or may not be of interest to you,
but I have decided to return to Juilliard in
the fall. Retirement does not suit me.
It would not surprise me one bit if you
were finished with violin. The industry
may very well be finished with you. As you
know, it is not a forgiving or generous one.
However, I do not love the industry or the
people in it. I love music. And it would be
a terrible thing for music if you were to let
scandal and humiliation force you from it.
I understand that up until a week ago you
were enrolled for the fall semester. I would
suggest you rethink your decision to
withdraw.

Sincerely,
Dr. Nanette Laroche

I glanced up at Jeremy. He was still doing the crossword puzzle, squinting and tapping his pencil on the
table's edge. All around me people were chattering,

licking frosting off their fingers, laughing. Staying here would be easy. I'd stay at Gigi's and run on the beach and be with Jeremy between tours. I'd be happy.

I reread the email, and felt the flicker of something inside of me. Something new. I had a choice.

Acknowledgments

Thank you to my agent, Mandy Hubbard, and my editor, Anica Rissi, for being so amazing at what you do and fun to work with too. I kind of want to be you guys when I grow up (and yes, I know we're all pretty close to the same age). And thanks to everyone else at Simon Pulse who worked so hard for *Virtuosity*.

Thanks to my siblings—Amanda, Steven, David, Michael, and Joshua—for keeping it real. You people are hilarious and smart and inspiring all at the same time.

Amy Hillis, *Virtuosity*'s first reader and friend extraordinaire, you convinced me I was a writer when I wasn't too sure, and then you watched my kids and forced me to go to that writing conference when I wanted to chicken out. You rule for that and for so many other things.

A special thanks to the violin teachers who have shaped my life: Edmond Agopian, Danuta Ciring, Igor Gruppman, Nick Pulos, Gwen Hoebig, Lorand Fenyves, and all the other musicians who have shared their talents with me.

Thank you Serge and Linda Martinez for loving me like one of your own.

Beth Tingle and Andrea Bingham, thank you for your lifelong friendship. Nobody else may have thought so, but the three of us together were hysterically funny at age seven. Ditto for age seventeen. Ditto for now.

And a shout-out to Olivia and Emily, my fabulous mother's helpers. My kids love you, and so do I! This book would've taken much longer to write without you. Keep reading, girls.

And finally, Mark. Thank you for making me laugh when I'm about to cry, and for always knowing the right thing to say. You . . . complete me. Just kidding. No, you really do, though.

SOME SECRETS
ARE TOO BIG TO KEEP.

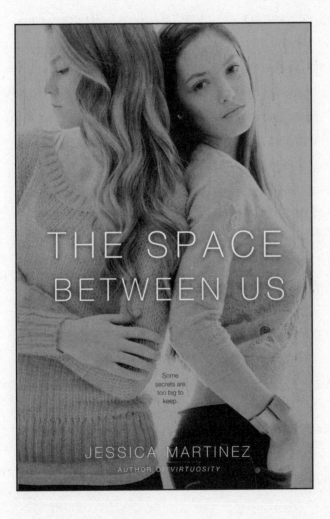

**THE SPACE
BETWEEN US**

Some
secrets are
too big to
keep.

JESSICA MARTINEZ
AUTHOR OF *VIRTUOSITY*

The truth just might tear them apart.

From
THE SPACE BETWEEN US
by Jessica Martinez

harlotte Mercer, please report to Principal
Blackburn's office. *Charlotte Mercer* to Principal Blackburn's office."

Static crackled, then the PA system cut out. I could
feel all twenty-two heads turn, but I kept my eyes on my
paper and gripped my pencil just a little tighter. Even Mr.
Mason stopped taking the derivative on the board and
glanced over his shoulder at me.

I forced myself to keep writing. *Move along, nothing to
see here.* As it was, the minute class was over I'd be fielding
questions about what she'd done. Like I knew.

Mr. Mason went back to the problem on the board,

and one by one, the weight of the stares lifted.

Please don't be another frog.

Last week she'd taken a huge bite out of one of the formaldehyde-soaked frogs in the biology lab. She couldn't have just nibbled off a tiny piece and spit it out. No, of course not. Apparently the dare stipulated chewing and swallowing, and Charly took her dares seriously. With half the class watching, she'd sunk her teeth into its torso, ripped off the entire left leg, then chewed and swallowed.

When Ms. Dansk realized what'd happened, she freaked out and sent Charly to the nurse, who determined Charly was physically fine (psychology report pending) and sent her along to Principal Blackburn. The whole thing resulted in a two-day in-school suspension for Charly and an hour-long assembly about lab safety for the entire school. Oddly enough, people were so impressed by the whole repulsive stunt, they weren't even mad about having to sit through the assembly.

Charly missed it. Dentist appointment.

I wasn't ready for another incident. I'd just decided I was going to hit the next person to ask me what frog tasted like.

The bell rang and Savannah met me at the doorway with an arched eyebrow. She knew better than to ask, but I answered anyway. "I have no idea. Let's go eat."

"Hey, Amelia," someone yelled from behind as we

pushed through bodies packing the hall. "Why's Charly in the office?"

"Don't know," I called without turning around.

Dean met us at the top of the stairwell, looking like someone stole his puppy. "Is she getting busted for the toaster oven thing?"

"What toaster oven thing?"

He glanced around for teachers. "You know . . . the toaster oven in the staff room . . ." He fiddled with the button on his shirt pocket and frowned, clearly trying to decide whether telling me was ratting her out or not.

Dean is one of a hundred guys at Primrose High who would follow Charly to the ends of the earth if he thought there was a chance she might accidentally touch his arm or something. The only difference between Dean and the others is that Charly actually likes him. It's the platonic sort of like she reserves for the cute, clean-cut boys, but it's enough for me to make a point of putting up with him.

"I have no idea what you're talking about and I don't care. Are you coming to lunch?"

He hesitated.

"Come on, baby face. She'll probably show up," I said. That did it.

The three of us sat at our usual table by the window with the scenic view of PHS's asphalt parking lot. Charly didn't show, but a handful of her minions did: Harrison,

Dean's slightly less intelligent wingman, Asha and Liam from drama club, and some tall guy with a dimpled chin whose name I can never remember.

"So what's the plan for homecoming?" Savannah asked between carrot sticks. For reasons unknown she'd bought a homecoming dress one size too small and stopped eating normal food. I'd already warned her the beta-carotene overload was going to turn her skin orange, but she didn't seem to care. Apparently super-skinny and orange was preferable to regular-skinny and human-colored.

"No plan for homecoming. I'm going to Atlanta with my dad," I said, eyeing the door. No Will yet, but it was Wednesday. He had debate team meetings on Wednesdays. Or he used to. Now Wednesdays were probably reserved for making out with Luciana in his car.

"We talking about homecoming?" Sebastian asked, putting his tray down next to Savannah. "Hey, sugar." He put his chin on top of her head and gave her a quick squeeze that looked disturbingly like a headlock.

"Hey, baby."

Sugar, baby, honey, cookie, sweetie pie. Good thing I was friends with them before they started going out. Otherwise I'd have to hate them for being so annoying.

"No, Savannah was talking about homecoming. I was talking about going to Atlanta."

"Enough of the too-cool-for-homecoming act,"

Savannah said. "You're not. And it's our senior year, so you have to come."

"Wrong. I don't. I've been the last three years. I already know exactly what happens. *You* have to go to collect your little princess tiara, but I am free to do whatever I want."

"So, why is your dad going to Atlanta?" Dean asked.

"He's giving some presentation at a conference."

Dean nodded and chewed slowly. "So, uh, your whole family's going?"

Poor Dean. It would be better if Charly was going to Atlanta so she wouldn't have to reject him outright again.

"No. Just me and my dad."

He took another bite of his sandwich and chewed with renewed enthusiasm. I was about to tell him to be careful not to bite his cheek or choke, when Savannah leaned over her tray and whispered, "You know that if you don't go to homecoming, *he* wins."

I glared into her big, concerned eyes. Could she not see the entire table full of people listening? "No. I really want to go to Atlanta. At the Coke museum they let you sample different Coke formulas from all over the world. Think of the buzz. A whole world of sugar and caffeine."

She sat up straight again. Then, rather than going along with my lame change-of-subject like any decent best friend would, she elbowed her puppet.

"Oh, yeah," Sebastian said, "I've got this friend I'm going to set you up with."

As if his brain produced its own thoughts in Savannah's presence. "I don't want to be set up with anyone."

"But you don't even know this guy," he argued. "He's cool."

I knew every man, woman, child, and dog in Tremonton. Very few of them could be classified as cool. "Where's he from?"

"Tallahassee. I roomed with him at soccer camp. And he'd just come from Bible camp too, so he probably wouldn't be too freaked out about your dad being a pastor."

I cringed. "If I was going to homecoming, a Tallahassee import would definitely have potential. But I'm not. Really. I'm going to Atlanta."

I hope. Dad had been noncommittal last time I brought it up, but he was more distracted than against it. He definitely didn't say "no."

So I'd started working on Grandma instead. I told her I wanted to research the Campus Missionary program for next year when I was at college, and what better place to start than the Southern Methodist Pastor's Conference? Plus I'd have plenty of downtime to work on my SAT prep book and do my homework. She'd been skeptical. She was *still* skeptical, but I had time to win her over, and as soon as she was on board, Dad would cave.

Atlanta was the perfect excuse to get out of town. I could spend the entire time studying by the pool and watching pay-per-view movies in the hotel room, both of which would be ten times more enjoyable than going to homecoming, or sitting at home thinking about previous homecomings.

Last year I went with Will. And the year before.

A group of skinny little freshman boys in baggy jeans with tough-guy chains shuffled up to the table.

"Hey, has your sister ever eaten roadkill?" the closest one asked.

I stared into the kid's eyes, trying not to be distracted by the whole face full of zits needing to be squeezed. Did he not realize I was a senior?

"Do you, um, think she'd eat roadkill if I dared her?" he continued. His friends had started to inch backward.

"Please go away." I turned back to my turkey sandwich.

"*Denied,*" one of the friends muttered as they wandered off.

Savannah pushed her plate of carrots aside and put a sympathetic hand on my arm. "Are you sure about homecoming?"

I closed my eyes, and willed myself to not flinch. She meant well. And she was right, if he showed up at homecoming with Luciana and I stayed away, I'd lose. People would assume I was sitting in front of a TV with a bag of powdered sugar mini-donuts.

But did it matter? They all assumed that *he* dumped *me* last April anyway.

"I'm sure," I said, and took a bite out of my apple.

Savannah didn't know why we'd broken up, and I couldn't explain it to her. I couldn't even explain it to Charly. And I was guessing the gorgeous Brazilian rebound didn't know either.

Will knew. And I knew.

"SHAZAM!" Charly's tray clattered as it hit the table across from me, fruit punch sloshing over the lip of her cup. She didn't notice. "I just survived a trip to Blackburn's cave."

I dropped a napkin on the juice spill. "Dare I ask why?"

"I put my bra on over top of my shirt after PE, and Senora Lopez freaked when she saw me in the hall."

"Why?"

"I don't know. Probably because she's mean and uptight."

"No. Why would you wear your bra over your shirt?"

She frowned. Clearly *why* had not come up yet. "Because I thought it would be funny. And it was, by the way."

"I'm sure Blackburn thought it was hilarious."

She put a fry in her mouth and grinned. "I told him I was protesting sweatshop labor in India and wherever else they make bras, and it was like he'd been hit by a tranquilizer dart. He started talking about protesting the Vietnam

War when he was young and some other crap I wasn't really listening to."

Dean and Harrison laughed. The thespians and the kid with no name followed, while Sebastian applauded. At least Savannah rolled her eyes.

"That's great," I said. "I'm sure all the little children hunched over sewing machines would be thrilled to know they've helped you out."

"And I will be forever grateful to them for saving me from an in-school suspension. He didn't even threaten to call home." She pulled the pieces of her grilled cheese apart and held one in front of my face. The mass of congealed orange cheese product was sweating. "Think this is organic?"

"Yeah," I said.

"Seriously? You think?" She wrinkled her nose.

"Of course not. Unless space age polymers are now falling under the organic label."

She closed the bread around the greasy cheese and took a bite.

"Since when do you care about eating organic?" Savannah asked suspiciously. She thinks she has dibs on living green since her stepdad bought her a hybrid. She's gone as far as to lecture strangers at the mall for tossing empty soda cans in the garbage.

"Since today," Charly answered. "Now that I'm a

protestor of sweatshop labor in . . . Amelia, where are the sweatshops?"

"China, Malaysia, Guatemala, the Philippines, Thailand . . . should I keep going?"

"No, that's good."

"Wait a second," Savannah jumped in, jabbing a finger dangerously close to my face. "You *can't* go to Atlanta. You guys have a big game! Ha!"

I knew it was only a matter of time until that hit her. "I'll have to miss it." The words felt wrong even as I said them. I'd never missed a field hockey game. Not even when I'd had mono.

"What? The team captain can't just skip out on the biggest game of the season."

"We'll beat Baldwin whether I'm here or not."

That wasn't true. I took another bite of my apple and stared at the core to avoid eye contact. Baldwin beat us last year, and was rumored to be even stronger this year. Something about a new German coach and brutal three-hour practices.

"What did Coach Hershey say?" Charly asked.

I glared at her. Whose side was she on? "I haven't told her yet. Today. At practice."

Coach Hershey is like a stick of dynamite: small, tightly packed, and deadly. I was still trying to come up with the right way of phrasing it so she wouldn't explode in my face.

"Homecoming is about football," I said. "Nobody cares about girls' field hockey."

"Apparently not," Savannah muttered, and folded her arms.

"Hey, speaking of Baldwin," Charly said, "can you give me a lift out there tomorrow night?"

"Why, so you can spend the evening stealing stop signs?"

Charly had come away from her summer job mowing greens at Baldwin Country Club with a paycheck, a tan, and a pack of total morons she now hung out with. Most of them were dropouts or just going nowhere. Unless there was a possibility of keg stands—then they were definitely going *there*.

"We didn't steal them. We borrowed them and then we put them back. Mostly."

"I won't even be home from practice until after five and then I've got homework. Plus, I need to practice for my choir audition."

She closed her eyes and shuddered. "You should *not* be auditioning for choir."

"I'm doing choir."

"But you have a terrible voice. No offense."

Sebastian and No-Name stifled laughs. Savannah coughed.

"Thanks a lot, guys," I muttered, then turned back to

Charly. "Offense taken, and I know I don't have the best voice, but choir will make me look well-rounded."

"But you're not."

"Conversation over."

"Does that mean you're not driving me to Baldwin?"

"You need to get your driver's license."

That shut her up. She'd already failed the road test twice.

"You don't want to go out to Baldwin tonight," Dean jumped in. "They're the enemy. Come with us to DQ after football."

If Charly answered, I didn't catch it. I was too busy watching Will.

He was coming through the doorway to the cafeteria, Luciana in tow, her pearly pink nails and brown skinny fingers curled around his biceps. He was talking, and she was laughing. No, her whole body was laughing—her head thrown back and her other hand touching her throat.

Please. Will is a lot of things, but he's not that funny.

Adrenaline screamed through my veins, but I didn't move. I gave myself three seconds. Three seconds to see how happy he looked, still tall and skinny, those same brown eyes and curly brown hair. Three miserable seconds, then I looked down.

Thankfully, Savannah was too busy canoodling with Sebastian to notice. Her sympathy is my kryptonite.

Charly pushed her pudding cup toward me. "Butter-scotch. You can have it."

She gave me a crooked half-smile, crooked because when we were ten she'd been standing on the wrong side of my swing during a softball game.

Butterscotch is her favorite.

"Thanks."

About the Author

JESSICA MARTINEZ lives in Orlando, Florida, with her husband, her two children, and her violin. She spends her days writing, running, and teaching her children to be music lovers too. Her novels include *Virtuosity* and *The Space Between Us*. Find out more at jessicamartinez.com.

Love. Heartbreak.
Friendship. Trust.

Fall head over heels for
Terra Elan McVoy.

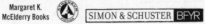

SiMONTEEN

Simon & Schuster's **Simon Teen**
e-newsletter delivers current updates on
the hottest titles, exciting sweepstakes, and
exclusive content from your favorite authors.

Visit **TEEN.SimonandSchuster.com** to
sign up, post your thoughts, and find out what
every avid reader is talking about!